Henry Dombey/FACECOLLECTIVE

Andrew Sean Greer is the author of the national bestseller *The Confessions of Max Tivoli*, as well as *How It Was for Me*, and one previous novel, *The Path of Minor Planets*. His stories have appeared in *The New Yorker*, *Esquire*, and *The Paris Review*. He has been the recipient of an NEA Fellowship, a California Book Award, and a New York Public Library Young Lions Award, as well as a Cullman Fellowship.

"Modern readers of literary fiction are a savvy bunch, usually able to spot a plot twist a mile away; however, Andrew Sean Greer has carried off not one but two shocks in his accomplished novel *The Story of a Marriage*."

—Charlotte Sinclair, *Vogue*

"This is a haunting book of breathtaking beauty and restraint. Greer's tone-perfect prose conjures an unforgettable woman who exists both within and somehow above the stifling class, racial, and sexual constraints of 1950s America—and who must unravel the great mystery of her place within it."

—Dave Eggers, author of *A Heartbreaking Work of Staggering Genius* and *What Is the What*

"*The Story of a Marriage* is a riveting and fascinating novel full of stunning observations and brilliant moments of truth and sympathy. It is written in prose that makes you want to slow the book down and read passages over again, but it also has a plot that makes you want to race ahead and stay up all night until you know what happens in the end."

—Colm Tóibín, author of *The Master*

"Andrew Sean Greer writes with an aching clarity of the heart. This is an exquisite story with shattering realizations about love. The details of a marriage between strangers are so finely observed that I often paused to wonder, How does he know so much?"

—Amy Tan, author of *The Joy Luck Club* and *Saving Fish from Drowning*

"For once, the publicity superlatives are true. *The Story of a Marriage* is a wonderful, exquisitely written book of the kind that keeps the reader up late at night to find out what happens next. . . . [A] truly touching, thought-provoking novel."

—Melissa McClements, *Financial Times* (UK)

"This emotionally complex novel resists tidy conclusions through finely nuanced narrative ambiguity and a bewitching lyricism." —Patrick Denman Flanery, *The Times Literary Supplement* (UK)

"A beautiful, understated novel that celebrates the heroes of private battles. It is peopled with those who have opted out— draft dodgers, conscientious objectors, and people on the margins of society who believe they are fighting for enough already, without taking on their nation's conflicts."

—Francesca Segal, *The Observer* (UK)

"An ambitious novel that examines postwar America through the prism of a complicated love triangle. *The Story of a Marriage* is designed to test your assumptions at every turn. It is clever, and Andrew Sean Greer's lush prose demands to be savored." —*Big Issue* (UK)

"As sculpted, trimmed, and polished as a perfect wood carving . . . If Andrew Sean Greer has manipulated his readers by first manipulating his protagonist, using all the trickery of novel writing, we can forgive him: he's produced a little master-piece." —Chris Dolan, *The Herald* (UK)

"Greer seamlessly choreographs an intricate narrative that speaks authentically to the longings and desires of his characters. . . . A tender kaleidoscope of both our history and Pearlie's heart."

—S. Kirk Walsh, *The New York Times*

THE STORY OF A MARRIAGE

The Story of a Marriage

ANDREW SEAN GREER

PICADOR

A FRANCES COADY BOOK

FARRAR, STRAUS AND GIROUX • NEW YORK

THE STORY OF A MARRIAGE. Copyright © 2008 by Andrew Sean Greer. All
rights reserved. Printed in the United States of America. For information,
address Picador, 175 Fifth Avenue, New York, N.Y. 10010.

www.picadorusa.com

Picador® is a U.S. registered trademark and is used by Farrar, Straus and
Giroux under license from Pan Books Limited.

For information on Picador Reading Group Guides, please contact Picador.
E-mail: readinggroupguides@picadorusa.com

Library of Congress Cataloging-in-Publication Data

Greer, Andrew Sean.
  The story of a marriage / Andrew Sean Greer. — 1st Picador ed.
    p. cm.
  ISBN-13: 978-0-312-42828-0
  ISBN-10: 0-312-42828-6
  1. Housewives—Fiction. 2. Husband and wife—Fiction. 3. Triangles
(Interpersonal relations)—Fiction. 4. Gay men—Fiction. 5. San Francisco
(Calif.)—Fiction. 6. Psychological fiction. I. Title.
  PS3557.R3987S76 2009
  813'.54—dc22

                                                                2008048081

First published in the United States by Farrar, Straus and Giroux

First Picador Edition: April 2009

10 9 8 7 6 5 4 3 2 1

For David Ross

I

*W*e think we know the ones we love.

Our husbands, our wives. We know them—we are them, sometimes; when separated at a party we find ourselves voicing their opinions, their taste in food or books, telling an anecdote that never happened to us but happened to them. We watch their tics of conversation, of driving and dressing, how they touch a sugar cube to their coffee and stare as it turns white to brown, then drop it, satisfied, into the cup. I watched my own husband do that every morning; I was a vigilant wife.

We think we know them. We think we love them. But what we love turns out to be a poor translation, a translation we ourselves have made, from a language we barely know. We try to get past it to the original, but we never can. We have seen it all. But what have we really understood?

One morning we awaken. Beside us, that familiar sleeping body in the bed: a new kind of stranger. For me, it came in 1953. That was when I stood in my house and saw a creature merely bewitched with my husband's face.

Perhaps you cannot see a marriage. Like those giant heavenly bodies invisible to the human eye, it can only be charted by its gravity, its pull on everything around it. That is how I think of it. That I must look at everything around it, all the hidden stories, the unseen parts, so that somewhere in the middle—turning like a dark star—it will reveal itself at last.

The story of how I met my husband; even that's not simple. We met twice: once in our Kentucky hometown, and once on a beach in San Francisco. It was a joke for our whole marriage, that we were strangers twice.

I was a teenager when I fell in love with Holland Cook. We grew up in the same farming community, where there were plenty of boys to love—at that age I was like those Amazonian frogs, bright green, oozing emotion from every pore—but I caught no one's eye. Other girls had boys falling over them, and although I did my hair just like them and ripped the trim off attic dresses and sewed it on my hems, it did no good. My skin began to feel like clothing I had outgrown; I saw myself as tall and gawky; and as no one ever told me I was beautiful—neither my mother nor my disapproving father—I decided that I must be plain.

So when a boy came along who actually met my eyes, who showed up along my walk from school and got himself invited in for a slice of bread, I didn't know what to make of him. I could tell he wanted something. For some reason I thought it was help on his schoolwork, so I always went to great pains to hide my notebooks and not sit next to him in class; I wouldn't be used like a crib sheet. But of course that wasn't what he wanted; he was always good in school. He never said what he wanted, in fact, not in all the years I knew him, but you do not judge a man by what he says. You judge him by what he does, and one clear bright night in May when we walked by the strawberry patch, he held my hand all the way to Childress. That's all it took, just the briefest touch, in those days when I wore my nerves outside my skin like lace. Of course I lost my heart.

I was there with Holland in World War Two. He loved that I "talked like a book" and not like any of the other girls, and when the time finally came for him to go into the army, I watched him step onto that bus and head to war. It was a lonely grief for a young girl.

It never occurred to me that I could leave as well, not until a government man walked up to our house and asked for me by name. I tromped down in my faded sundress to find a very ruddy and clean-shaven man wearing a lapel pin of the Statue of Liberty in gold; I coveted it terribly. His name was Mr. Pinker. He was the kind of man you were supposed to obey. He talked to me about jobs in California, how industries wanted strong women like me. His words—they were rips in a curtain, revealing a vista to a world I had never imagined before: airplanes, California; it was like agreeing to travel to another planet. After I thanked the man, he said, "Well then, as thanks you can do a favor for me." To my young mind, it seemed like nothing special at all.

"Now that sounds like the first bright idea you *ever* had," my father said when I mentioned leaving. I can't find any memory in which he held my gaze as long as he did that day. I packed my bags and never saw Kentucky again.

On the bus ride to California, I studied the mountains' ascent into a line of clouds and saw where, as if set upon those clouds, even higher mountains loomed. I had never seen a sight like that in all my life. It was as if the world had been enchanted all along and no one told me.

As for the favor the man asked of me, it was perfectly simple: he just wanted me to write letters. About the girls around me in the shipyard and the planes and conversations I overheard, everyday rituals: what we ate, what I wore, what I saw. I laughed to think what good it would do him. Now I can only laugh at myself—the government must have been looking for suspicious activities, but he didn't tell me that. He told me to pretend I was keeping a diary. I did my duty; I did it even when I left my first job to become a WAVE—only a few other girls from a community like mine—spreading Noxzema on our pimply faces, the girls' rears shaking to the radio, getting used to Coke instead of rationed coffee and Chinese food instead of hamburgers. I sat there every night and tried to write it all down, but I found my own life lacking; it hardly seemed worth telling. Like so many people, I was deaf to my own stories. So I made them up.

My life wasn't interesting to me, but I'd read books that were, and that is what I put down, with details stolen from Flaubert and Ford and Ferber, intrigues and sorrows and brief colorful joys: a beautiful work of fiction for my country held together with si- lence and lies. That is, it turns out, what holds a country together. I did my job well, in the handwriting my mother had taught me, tall and loyal and true, signed with the special slipknot *P* for Pearlie I invented at the age of nine, mailed to Mr. William Pinker, 62 Holly Street, Washington, D.C.

What did you do in the war, Grandma? I lied to my country, pretending to tattle on friends. I'm sure I was just one of thou- sands; I'm sure it was a clearinghouse for lonely hearts like me. Imagine the ad jingle: "Be a finker . . . for Mr. Pinker!"

Then the war ended, as did the factory work for women and our jobs as WAVEs. I had long since stopped writing my notes to Wash- ington; there was so much else to worry about and I had my posi- tion doing piecework sewing to pay for meals. And one day, alone down by the ocean, I walked right by a sailor on a bench, sitting with his book facedown like a fig leaf on his lap, staring out to sea.

I knew very little about men, so I was startled to see such de- spair on his square handsome face. I knew him. The boy who'd held my hand all the way to Childress, whose heart I had, at least briefly, possessed. Holland Cook.

I said hello.

"Well hi there, Sarah, how's the dog?" he said amiably. The wind stopped, as if, like Holland, it did not recognize me. Sarah was not my name.

We stayed there for a moment in the oyster-colored air, with his smile slowly sagging, my hand holding the flap of my coat to my throat, my bright kerchief tugging in the wind, and a sickness building in my stomach. I could have moved on; merely walked away so he would never know who I was. Just some strange girl fading into the fog.

But instead I said my name.

Then you recognized me, didn't you, Holland? Your childhood sweetheart. Pearlie who'd read poetry to you, who'd taken piano lessons from your mother; that was the second time we met. A sudden memory of home, opening like a pop-up book. He chatted with me, he even made me laugh a little, and when I said I had no escort to the movies that Friday and asked if he would come, he paused a while before looking at me, saying quietly, "All right."

I was shocked when he turned up at my rooming house. The low-watt bulbs revealed a weary man, hat in his hands, his skin a little ashen, his elegant necktie loosely knotted. He claimed, years later, that he couldn't even remember what he or I wore that night: "Was it the green dress?" No, Holland; it was black roses on white; its pattern is framed and hung in my memory alongside our honeymoon wallpaper (pale green garlands). I thought he might be drunk; I was afraid he might collapse, but he smiled and offered his arm and after the film took me to a nice restaurant out in North Beach. At dinner, he hardly ate or spoke. He barely looked at me, or noticed the stares we got from other patrons; his own gaze was fixed on two cast-iron dogs that sat before the un-lit fireplace. So after we had taken the streetcar to my corner, and it was time to say good night, I was surprised when he turned very quickly and kissed me on the mouth. An electric jolt of happiness passed through me. He stepped back, breathing quickly and but-toned his jacket to go. "I have to see a friend," he told me sharply.

"Holland," I said. He looked back at me as if I had jerked a string. "Holland," I repeated. He waited. And then I said the right thing. It was the only time I ever did: "Let me take care of you."

His deep eyes awakened. Did he think I meant to remind him of our time back in Kentucky, that I offered the soft threat of the past? A dark line appeared between his eyebrows.

He said, "You don't know me, not really."

I told him that didn't matter, but what I meant was that he was wrong; I knew him, of course I knew all about him from that time in our constricting little hometown: the grass behind the school-yard we used to poke with a stick, the path from Franklin to Childress cluttered with witch hazel and touch-me-nots and railroad vine, the ice shivering in a summer pitcher of his mother's lemonade—the lost world that only I remembered. For here we were so far from home. The one we could never regain. Who could know him better than I?

I acted instinctively. All I wanted was to keep him there on the shining streetcar tracks. "Let me take care of you again."

"You serious?" he asked.

"You know, Holland, I've never been kissed by any boy but you."

"That ain't true, it's been years, Pearlie. So much has changed."

"I haven't changed."

Immediately he took my shoulder and pressed his lips to mine.

Two months later, by those same cable-car tracks, he whispered: "Pearlie, I need you to marry me." He told me that I didn't really know his life, and of course he was right. Yet I married him. He was too beautiful a man to lose and I loved him.

The first thing people noticed in my husband was his looks. Tall, dark, with a comforting smile that seemed to hide nothing: the kind of effortless beauty that cannot be marred by strain or illness, like something beaten out of gold, so that even if you bent it or melted it down it would always be a pure, beautiful thing. That's how I saw him, ever since I was a girl staring at him in our class-room. But I was not alone; it was how everybody saw him.

Beauty is a warping lens. He had the kind of looks that are always greeted by grins and handshakes, extra glances, stares held for a moment longer than usual; a smile and a face not easily forgotten. Even the way he held a cigarette, or leaned over to tie his shoe, had a certain masculine grace that made you want to sketch him. What a distorted, confusing way to live. To be offered jobs and rides and free drinks—"It's on the house, sweetie"—to sense a room changing as you move through it. Watched everywhere you go. To be someone people long to possess, and to be used to this feeling; to be wanted so immediately, so often, that you have never known yourself what you might want.

And he was mine, of all incredible things.

What would I have told you about my husband, in those young days of our marriage? Just that he had a lovely baritone. And liked his whiskey neat. That he would lend a stranger twenty dollars if he seemed like the right sort of fellow; and later, when we had a son, he carefully tracked his health, and called the doctor whenever we were worried, and tenderly soaped Sonny's legs in the bathtub as if everything were good. Always well dressed and smelling of leather and wood, like a favorite coat or a fine piece of furniture. He liked to smoke but hated to be seen doing it—a holdover from his soldier days—and I would come upon him, in our married home, leaning against the frame of the patio door with a lonely expression, right hand dangling emptily inside, left hand trailing smoke: exactly the position of California leaning against the Pacific. He kissed me goodbye every morning at eight and hello every evening at six; he worked hard to provide for us all; he had nearly lost his life for his country. Loyal, decent, a soldier: American virtues. All that is true, of course, though it gets no closer to the real man. They are simply the things one would set upon a tombstone. They have, in fact, been set upon the tombstone of Holland Cook.

Just after our engagement, Holland's aunts arrived at my rooming house. Alice and Beatrice, not really his aunts, in fact, but elderly twin cousins who, when he came to San Francisco, announced they were his mothers now, and arranged themselves in his life like cats unhelpfully placing themselves in the folds of an unmade bed.

They took me out for an elegant lunch and they told me that I needed to know something about Holland before I married him. It was a beautiful setting. We sat in a special area of a department-store lunchroom, after being turned away by two others; it was four floors up from Union Square with a great stained-glass ship floating overhead and waiters, old men in jackets, buzzing everywhere, back in the days when department stores had rotunda art galleries and libraries of books to buy or rent. Imagine a time when you could rent a book from Macy's! I sat in that glittering room with those pinched old women staring at me with odd, sad expressions. I was young and scared to death. "We need to tell you about Holland," one of them said—I hadn't yet learned the trick to telling them apart—and the other nodded. "He's real ill. I'm sure he hasn't told you."

"He's ill?"

They shared a glance—I was too young to know what it might mean—and Alice said, "There isn't a cure."

"It's gotten better, but there isn't a cure," her twin repeated. I would later learn that the difference between them was that the elder had a birthmark, and the younger's heart had been broken, thirty years earlier, by a married man. As if that, too, might leave a mark.

I looked down and noticed I'd eaten all the beautiful popovers.

"He's had a hard life," Alice cut in, and it made no sense to me. "The war, his mother's death—" and then she broke off in a sob, staring out the great windows that looked down on a monument: Dewey's triumph in the Pacific.

I asked them what exactly was wrong with him. The younger aunt put her hand on her lips, like an old statue, and told me it was bad blood, a crooked heart, that there was no cure for it.

"But," I said, "but I'll take care of him."

"We heard how you took care of him in the war," Beatrice said.

"Yes," I told them carefully. "Yes, me and his mother."

She looked at me with a shrewd eye. I was at that age when you believe all kinds of upside-down things, including that your elders are innocents and fools, and that women in particular are children, to be treated gently and kindly, and only you—who have, after all, kissed a soldier back from war—know anything of the world. So while I heard those women speaking in their haughty accents, I was not really listening to the words.

"Miss Ash," the older aunt said and then used my first name: "Pearlie. We're relying on you. Don't you let him out of your sight. You know how he loves some excitement, and it'll kill him for sure. I don't like him taking our old property, out in the Outside Lands, it makes me nervous, but I guess it'll do him good, far away, out near the ocean air. He won't need to go downtown, or worry over the past. His family should be enough, Pearlie. You should be enough."

"Well of course." I could not guess what worry they meant. I was distracted by our waiter, a colored man, who was approaching, smiling at me, with a folded napkin in his hands. "I don't know about any old trouble. We aren't interested in frivolous things. That is not what he fought the war for." I spoke very carefully; I thought I'd mention his war experience, as a kind of proof against this idea of weakness.

Alice, though, had got quite worked up over something. She was inhaling in long, loud breaths like a cave at high tide and stared directly at the table in front of her. Her sister took her arm and she began to shake her head. Her jewelry blinked in the gray sunlight. Then she said something that I decided immediately I hadn't heard right, because it was so absurd, so crazed, and before I could get her to repeat it, we were interrupted. It was a friend of theirs, a woman in a fancy hat with a pheasant quill, asking the Misses Cook about the Daffodil Festival and whether they thought there would be more flowers this year or fewer. Fewer, it was decided, because of the winter weather. As they talked, the waiter arrived, opened his napkin before me, and presented, burnished as bronze armor, a pile of hot popovers. It was so good in those days to be young.

If you clenched your right hand in a fist, that would be my San Francisco, knocking on the Golden Gate. Your little finger would be sunny downtown on the bay, and your thumb would be our Ocean Beach out on the blue Pacific. They called it the Sunset. That's where we lived, with our son, in an old property set like a rough stone among the thousands of new houses put up for returning soldiers and their families, in a part of the city no one really built on until the war was over. Then hills were flattened; soil was laid down over the sand; and they built a grid of streets and low pastel houses with garages and Spanish roofs and picture windows that flashed with the appearance of the sun, all in rows for fifty avenues until you reached the ocean. It felt outside of everything. Once, the *Chronicle* published a map of nuclear damage to San Francisco if it were hit, with rings of rubble and fire. The Sunset was the only district to survive.

When we first moved in, there were so many empty lots that sand always glittered in the air, and it could bury a vegetable garden overnight. Above the sound of the ocean, one could sometimes hear the early-morning roar of the lions in the nearby zoo. It was nothing like the rest of the city, no hills or views or bohemians, nothing Italian or Victorian to make you take a photograph. A new way to live, separated from downtown by more than just a mountain with one tunnel. It sat on the very edge of the continent, with fog so dense and silver you hardly ever saw a sunset in the Sunset; any glowing light was often just a streetcar emerging like a miner from that tunnel, making its satisfied way out to the ocean.

It was a Saturday. It was 1953, and weeks before we had all watched on television as President Eisenhower and Richard Nixon were sworn in as the first government we could remember neither to be led nor haunted by FDR. We watched that inauguration, full of worries about the Korean War, race issues, the Rosenbergs, the Communists hidden everywhere around us, the Russian bombs being prepared and inscribed like voodoo charms with our names: Pearlie, Holland, Sonny. We watched. And told ourselves:

Help is coming.

People have an idea about the fifties. They talk about poodle skirts and bus strikes and Elvis; they talk about a young nation, an innocent nation. I don't know why they have it so wrong; it must be the consolidation of memory, because all that came later, as the country changed. In 1953, nothing had changed. We were still so haunted by the war. Fluoridation seemed like a horrible new invention, and the Woolworth's on Market a beautiful one. In those days, the firemen still wore leather helmets; William Platt the Seltzer Boy still left fizzing bottles on our doorstep, waking me with the ring of glass on concrete; the milkman still drove his old-fashioned wagon with gold script on the side—Spreckels Russell—and, impossible as it seems, the iceman still pulled blocks out with his medieval tongs like a dentist doing an extraction on a whale, making his rounds for those last households without a refrigerator. The rag man and the knife man, the fruit truck and the coal truck and the dry cleaners, the fish man and the Colonial Bread man and the egg lady—all came down the street with their echoing cries of "Rags bottles trash!" and "Grind your scissors! Grind your knives!"; a sound that's gone forever. No one had ever heard anything wilder than a big band, or seen a man grow his hair longer than his ears. We were still trying to figure out how to live in a war after a war.

It was a medieval time for mothers. When he was three, my boy, Sonny, was playing with his loving father in the backyard when I heard shouting. I came running to find my son collapsed in the bower vine. My husband picked him up, rocking him in his arms, hushing his frightened boy, telling me to call the doctor. In those days, they had no idea what caused polio or what to do. The doctor told me it was "brought on by summer"—a magical diagnosis for a city without a summer. His treatment was leg splints, bed rest, and hot towels, which I applied carefully, and our only other solace was church services where weeping mothers held up photographs of children. It wasn't a time of freshness and freedom. It was a time of dread; the war was easy compared to this. It's a wonder we didn't run screaming into the streets and set fire to one another's houses.

Instead, we hid our fears. Just as my mother hid a lock of her dead brother's hair in the throat of her high-collared Sunday dress, in a pocket she had sewn there. You cannot go around in grief and panic every day; people will not let you, they will coax you with tea and tell you to move on, bake cakes and paint walls. You can hardly blame them; after all, we learned long ago that the world would fall apart and the cities would be left to the animals and the clambering vines if grief, like a mad king, were allowed to ascend the throne. So what you do is you let them coax you. You bake the cake and paint the wall and smile; you buy a new freezer as if you now had a plan for the future. And secretly—in the early morning—you sew a pocket in your skin. At the hollow of your throat. So that every time you smile, or nod your head at a teacher meeting, or bend over to pick up a fallen spoon, it presses and pricks and stings and you know you've not moved on. You never even planned to.

"It is equal to living in a tragic land," a poet once wrote, "to live in tragic times."

Yet I have to admit I loved our house. I had chosen it, after all; in defiance of the aunts, I had pressed Holland to take that old Sunset property, and at first it was the fulfillment of our dreams. A house with a yard; a bedroom my son didn't have to share; carpets and folding blinds and even a place behind the bathroom mirror for Holland to drop his razor blades. It was a miracle: a house that had thought of everything before me. You could never have convinced me, back when I was young, that all the real moments of my life would happen in that vine-covered house, just as a telephone installer can't tell a young couple that their happiest and saddest news will come through that polished phone. It's hard to think, even now, that the sweet ebony milkmaid that Holland's aunts gave us in the first year of our marriage and that sat on the bookshelf would watch with its painted eyes every vital decision I ever made. So too the bamboo coffee table. And the "broken pot" that Sonny had made from a drinking glass, masking tape, and shellac. The yarn cat, the broken mantel clock. They watched the whole six months of that affair, and in the hour of my judgment they will surely be called together to account for things.

As for what Holland's aunt told me on that afternoon of tea and popovers, I had decided long before to forget it. Marriage was all that cluttered my mind, and the new house, and the care of my child. I could not pay attention to the memory of an old woman shouting, in her muffled voice:

"Don't do it! Don't marry him!"

· ᘯ

It was 1953. It was a Saturday.

Four years of happy marriage had passed, and the aunts were still in our lives. They'd grown stouter over time, and somehow their sharp-chinned heads seemed huger than ever, Duchesses from *Alice in Wonderland*, fussing with their enormous hats as they sat telling me a story at our kitchen table. Beneath it, hidden by the apple-red oilcloth, lay my little boy.

"Oh Pearlie, we forgot to tell you about the murder!" said Alice.

Beatrice was in the act of putting on her hat, pin in hand like a harpooner. "That terrible murder!"

"Yes," said her sister.

"You ain't heard?" asked Beatrice with a worried expression. "Up north?"

I shook my head and picked up the newspaper, holding my scissors aloft. Sunlight came in through the kitchen window, blurred by my son's fingerprints. It was two o'clock and a bicycle bell was still ringing in my ears.

"It was a murder, Pearlie—" Alice tried to interrupt.

"A woman trying to get a divorce—"

"This was up in Santa Rosa—"

Beatrice threw her hands up in air, hatpin whirling like a dragonfly, settling for a second, then darting away with her words. "Oh it happens all the time. She wanted a divorce from her two-timing husband. It isn't easy, as you know. She was up with one of those lawyers, up at their cabin where they knew the husband was hiding . . . with his . . . well you know . . ."

Her sister filled in the blank: "With his little bit on the side."

"His mistress, Pearlie, his mistress," announced Beatrice, not to be outdone.

Beatrice smiled at where my son hid under the table. He had been there for an hour, without a toy, without the dog (who lay at my feet); it was a wonderful mystery to me. My child who could be happy under a tablecloth. I remember thinking: *When the dishwasher's done, he'll come out.* The machine was an extravagance, a gift from the aunts. As they chatted, I stood and listened to it turning and murmuring beside me like a dream from which we would awaken.

I asked if it was a colored woman.

"A what? No, the wife was white and so was the mistress. I don't know why you'd think—"

"Anyhow," continued the elder twin, leaning in with the deliciousness of the story. She waved her hands and pointed down the hall to the front window, as if the scene had happened right here in this very house. "Anyhow, she and the detective and the photographer, they snuck up there to that cabin to take a photo. For divorce grounds, you see, she needed evidence of . . . of *adultery* . . . for divorce grounds. She needed a photo of the man and his—"

"And they broke in!" shouted Alice. "Camera flashing! And what do you know—"

"The man had a gun. He thought they were robbers." Now they were telling it together.

"Oh yes. Of course he did!"

"Who else would be breaking into his house?"

"Who else?"

"And then," Beatrice said as she set the straw hat on her head, "and then he shot his wife dead." She looked straight into my eyes. *"Shot her dead!"*

The pin went *crik* into the hat.

Said her sister: "Happens all the time!"

While they were telling their gruesome story, I sat in a coat-dress under a long window fringed from trailing vines; that was where I sat every day and censored my husband's paper. I had to finish before he got home from working overtime, had to leave him a paper with nothing but good news. It was one of the many things I took pride in doing for Holland's health; for his heart. It's easy to laugh at the aunts, but at that luncheon years before, when the younger one had become so upset—"Don't marry him!"—I believed they were trying to help me.

In my stubborn way, though, I had decided to defy those poor dears and do my best to keep Holland safe. They could not know what he meant to me, those women who had never had a husband.

And so my imagination, that incautious artist, created from her words of warning—"bad blood, a crooked heart"—the image of a transposed organ. I came to believe that was his illness. I pictured it like a slide shown in a darkened medical classroom: poor Holland, born with a defect, his heart hanging over on his right side like a cherry. I imagined a cutaway Holland with his insides fitting like a puzzle, a lecturer tapping on his rib cage: "Only one in ten thousand show the right-sided gene." It was a beautiful image to form my life around. I was proud of my extraordinary husband, and my extraordinary duties as a wife: to keep him safe and, even better, unaware of danger. Health is only enjoyed in the blithe ignorance that you will lose it. In that way it is like youth.

I took those duties seriously. With Holland's unspoken approval, I created an elaborate system meant to save his heart. First of all, I made the house a cloister of quiet; the telephone had a peculiar purr instead of a ring, and the front door hummed instead of clanging (you will hear it in a moment); I bought him an alarm clock that produced an erotic series of vibrations in the morning—I even went so far as to find a barkless dog. I read about the breed in the papers, and went to some lengths to find one. Sitting at my feet on the kitchen floor, eyes closed in pleasure at my mere presence, mute freckled Lyle. There was no need to keep our Sonny quiet; he was born quiet, as if he were the antidote to my husband's heart, and it was only me I had to keep in check; I never raised my voice. I knew instinctively that it would shake my husband, that it would go against everything I was sworn to in our marriage, and so I silenced everything in myself that wasn't mild and good.

So my task that Saturday was to pick up the day's paper and read over it before Holland might read something too violent, too shocking, that might break his tender transposed heart.

"To murder your own wife—" the eldest began again.

"Oh don't talk about it anymore, Beatrice. Not today. Not in front of the boy."

A wicked smile cut from the old lady. "I'm not sure I don't blame the wife!"

"Beatrice!"

. The sound of the streetcar came from down the street and both ladies automatically looked at their watches.

"We've got to run!" she answered. "We can't wait for Holland. I don't know why you let him give that DeLawn girl a ride. It's only trouble." At the mention of her name, I thought of that bicycle bell again.

"All our love, Pearlie," her sister said, adjusting her girdle.

"And you keep an eye on our Holland."

I asked Sonny to come out and say goodbye, but they shushed me and said it didn't matter; boys were just that way.

"Goodbye, darling," each said as she kissed me.

Two minutes and two kisses later we were left alone. Ten minutes after that, our own doorbell would ring—or coo, I should say, coo like a mourning dove—and our dog, Lyle, would leap into the air and I would open the door and there he would stand, the stranger: "Hello, ma'am, I hope you can help me." With those ordinary words, everything would change.

But for the moment, the world was still and quiet. All I could see of my son, under the table, were his shoes as motionless as brass things. I'm sure it was beautiful down there. Deep brown Marmoleum flooring shining like frozen mud, split in a few places where it met the cabinetry, beginning to wear right under the sink where he had watched me stand for countless hours before the rolling dishwasher (a monster) arrived, watched me stand in my seamed stockings. In those days I wore stockings with gold diamonds at the ankle with a *P* (for Pearlie), and that was all he could see of me, just those gold diamonds, which are among the few memories he has kept of me from his childhood.

Those shoes, the left larger than the right. They had been a gift from his "shoe buddy" in Montana. The March of Dimes worked very hard to help us, and found a boy with polio whose mismatched feet were exactly the opposites of Sonny's. Whenever we went shopping, we always bought two pairs of shoes, keeping the smaller left and the larger right, and sending the others off to little John Garfield from Montana. We always enclosed a letter, and John's mother always wrote back sending shoes she had bought for her son. It was a neat arrangement. In fact, John and my son were "shoe buddies" until they were teenagers, fully recovered, and by the time they were grown the draft doctors could hardly tell they had ever been stricken, and, remarkable as it seems, approved them both for the army. War changes so many young men. My son fled up to Canada, and we later heard that poor patriotic John went off and died in Vietnam, far away from his beloved Rocky Mountains.

From the street-side window came a throat-clearing sound. Lyle belatedly leaped up from his coil on the floor and jerked his head around like a windup thing. His mute little mouth opened an inch, with that hopeful look that dogs get, little suppliants in fur, and I reached down and scratched his ears.

We all sat still as statues. From the window drifted sweet music: a child's first piano-lesson plunkings of a church song. A mayfly on the window stroked the glass as if it were putting a baby to sleep. Then, at last, the dishwasher moaned and released its load of gray water into the sink.

Now he'll come out, I thought.

And out he came, my little boy: three feet tall and nothing but denim slacks and a terry T-shirt with WALTER WALTER WALTER stitched all over it, a gift from the aunts, his favorite shirt though we never called him "Walter," never called him anything but Sonny; bright eyes in a bright face, his tongue stained by the berries he'd been eating—some wonderful creature sent to live with me. I called his name and he smiled. I would do anything for him.

Whirr went the doorbell. The dog leaped into the air.

I took off my apron and followed Lyle into the hall, where I could see—partly eclipsing the door's round window—the blurry peak of a man's hat. I winked as I looked back at my son. I gave him one last wave before I opened the door.

He was the most unlikely caller. We had no regular visitors, certainly none this neatly and elegantly dressed, from the shine of the wet-combed hair showing from under his hat to the shine of his wing-tip shoes. As I opened the door, his head was bowed, as if listening for something, and I had time to examine the twin peaks of his high forehead, slightly damp with sweat, the curves of his Scottish cheekbones, and it was only when he heard my greeting and raised his head that I noticed the break in his nose. Right there, like a boxer's, giving him the exciting air of someone who had touched danger. His eyes, however, were very calm and friendly. Perfectly sapphirine.

The stranger looked up at me as if he were surprised to see me, yet pleased. He smiled and said he hoped I could help him.

I said I hoped so, too. He was holding two small presents.

"I wonder . . . I seem to be lost," he said.

I asked if he was visiting town.

"That's the funny part. In a foreign city, I'm never lost. Something about the survival instinct." A wide, chuckling grin. "But here in my own town . . ."

I leaned my body against the doorframe. I smiled and said nothing. I noticed the DeLawn girl's pink bicycle fallen where she always left it, lying on the lawn as if it had been wounded in battle.

He removed his hat. I wasn't very used to men like him removing their hats in my presence. His hair was gold. I asked the name of the street he was looking for.

"It's a Spanish name. Maybe I should pretend I'm in Spain, that might help."

I said he might not be lost after all.

"Is this Noriega?" he asked.

In a soft voice, I said, "Yes."

"Is it? Then I'm not doing half bad. I've never been to this neighborhood before. I didn't know people lived so close to the ocean. Like a South American beach town."

"They used to call it the Outside Lands," I said.

He smiled. "The Outside Lands." He seemed familiar, something in the way he dressed and held himself, but perhaps it was just the touch of the South in his voice, so far from home. What I remember more clearly than any of the rest was how he stared right at me the whole time he talked with me. It wasn't something I was used to, in my neighborhood, where even the seltzer boy could barely meet my eye. Right at me, with those startling eyes. As if he had finally found the person who would listen.

"Who are you looking for?"

He set down the presents and pulled off his gloves, then produced a notebook where a number had been written in what I could see was a careful, schoolboy scrawl. It was then I noticed his missing finger. His left little finger. But you saw that all the time in those days; every young soldier had lost something in the war.

Still looking at the notebook, he read aloud a number that I knew by heart. It was painted on the curb but hidden by a car.

I said, "Holland Cook."

"Yes, you know him?"

Across the street I could see my neighbor Edith crossing her picture window and looking out, taking in everything at a glance so she could discuss it later as she stood with her friends in the warm, crisp smell of her ironing machine. The piano lesson floated by in halting notes. From one of a dozen windows came the sound of a television, chattering to itself: "The story of a girl and the man who tries to learn her identity, watch for the unexpected ending . . ."

"I'm his wife."

To my astonishment, he grinned and put out his hand. "Well you must be Pearlie."

I asked if he was from the army.

"Am I . . . ?"

"From the army," I said. "You look like a government man."

"Is it the clothes?"

I shrugged. "The shoes."

"Of course. No, I'm not from the government," he said, "but I did know your husband in the war."

"First Infantry?"

He gave a painful smile and dropped his hand, though he didn't remove his eyes from my face, not for an instant. "I'm sorry to bother you," he said. "Looks like you got things to do this morning." I realized I had a pair of scissors in my hand, and I dropped them into a pocket of my coatdress. I heard Sonny making his way down the hall. With his legs in their braces, he sounded like the Tin Woodsman. "That must be your son," the man said.

I said it was, and turned to Sonny, who was hiding behind a console. "Baby, say hello to the man."

"Hi there, my name's Buzz Drumer."

"Say hello to Mr. Drumer," I said, but Sonny did nothing. "He's usually chatty."

"He's a beauty, like his mother."

This startled me. Sonny was a beauty, of course—"made from gingerbread," I always whispered to him in the morning—but I assumed his looks came from his father, that my husband's genes, like alchemical agents, could not be dulled by my own. It would never have occurred to me that my son's eyes—more honeyed than Holland's—might be anything but a gift of nature; might be mine, for example. "Oh he's a handful," was all I said.

"It must be hard."

I could not imagine what he expected me to say.

"I mustn't keep you," he said. "I wonder if you could pass this on to Holland. Just something, well, I knew his birthday was coming up."

"It's next month."

"Oh yes, that's right," he said, shaking his head. "I don't keep dates in my head too well. All the numbers run together. Just names and faces, the important things."

I said nobody ever minded an early present.

"And it's your birthday, too, ain't it?" he asked, smiling.

I couldn't think how a stranger might know my birthday.

"They're a day apart, right? I hear in China that's lucky for the woman. I hope I got that right, at least, because I got something for you—"

"You didn't need to do that," I said, unreasonably flattered and confused.

He nodded. "It's how my mama raised me. Will Holland be home soon?"

For a brief mad moment I considered lying. Maybe it was the fog so low and soft over everything, or his eyes flashing that peculiar shade of blue, or because I could hear something in his voice, something more than what he was saying.

But I couldn't stand in a doorway and lie to a stranger.

"Yes," I said. "Yes, he should be home any minute."

"I knew Holland would marry a beautiful girl. Well, anyone could guess that. You're his childhood sweetheart, isn't that right? He talked about you all the time."

An elderly German neighbor-woman had come out of her house to stare at us. I stepped aside and said, "Would you like to come in and wait?"

We sat a few feet apart on the sofa, and he happily drank a beer as I stroked Lyle's ears. He told me stories about the younger Holland, his employee at one point, and said over and over how it was sure nice to meet me; I was exactly the kind of girl he'd always thought Holland would marry. Beautiful; he kept saying I was beautiful; it was as strange as someone telling me I was French. Eventually he forced his present into my hand—a little turquoise box no bigger than a slice of toast. I refused it at first.

He had that way of trying to be too close to people too soon. But Buzz was a charmer, yes he was, and at last he coaxed me into opening it.

"Thank you, how beautiful."

Five minutes later, the wrapping paper lay between us on the couch. I felt Lyle's tail thumping against my leg; it was the loving premonition of Holland's arrival. We heard the front door open, and then my husband appeared on the steps of our sunken living room. Lyle ran to him and we both stood as if in the presence of royalty.

Down he came, my husband. We watched as parts of Holland stepped into the circle of light, beginning with the polished wing tip of one leather shoe, then the second, and then the creased trouser cuffs of a suit, long legs in charcoal wool, a belt around the still-trim waist of a high-school track star, an uncharacteristically rumpled dress shirt, rolled up to show his forearms and the twin gleams of his watch and his wedding ring—"Hello? Hello?"—and then that face that I so loved, my husband's dark astonished face.

"Hi there, sweetheart," I said. "You got an old friend visiting."

Holland stood very still, startled, hands open like a saint as his son and dog ran toward him. He was staring at Buzz. I watched as the look burned into something like contempt. Then he stared at me. For some reason he looked afraid.

"Hi Holland," Buzz said. He stood there with his arms out in greeting.

As my husband turned back to his friend, I recognized what had seemed so familiar about this man at the door: he dressed like my husband. The tweed coat and foldable hat and long sleek trousers, even the way he rolled his shirtsleeves double up to just below the elbow. It was how Holland had always dressed since the war. And in a moment you could see that my husband, choosing his clothing so carefully from the stores we could afford, marching with a sale-rack tie over to the discontinued shirts, worrying over a scarf, was just a make-do version of this man's style. And what I had taken as a personal touch, an extension of my husband's general beauty, turned out to be an imitation. Like a reconstruction of a lost portrait, an imitation of a subject I had not seen until that day.

He turned to his old friend. "Hi there, Buzz," he said evenly. "What are you doing here?"

"Just popped in my mind to drop by. Your wife is a beauty."

"Pearlie, this is Mr. Charles Drumer, who was my boss—"

I said, "Yes, he told me."

The two men regarded each other warily for a moment more. My husband said, "It's been a long time."

Buzz said, "A few years."

Holland's eyes dropped to the carpet where a piece of blue paper, torn in the shape of a lost continent, had fallen. I said Buzz had brought me a present, and he looked startled. There it lay on a bed of tissue on the table. "Did he?"

A pair of gloves, in white. It wasn't until Buzz had encouraged me to try them on that I'd noticed, embroidered on the right-hand palm, a small red bird, tail high in the air, wings out, as if it had just been caught. If you stretched your hand, the creature would writhe in your palm like a living thing.

"Bird in the hand!" I said merrily to Holland, showing the bird to him, making it move.

"Bird in the hand," Buzz repeated, hands in his pockets.

Holland, my old husband—you looked from me to your lost friend and back again. What did you see there? What went through your tender mind? We were certainly a strange pair to find standing in your living room. The last thing you expected. And then, of all wonderful things, you began to laugh.

No woman would ever refer to someone she lost touch with as "a good friend," yet men will drop and pick up friends as cavalierly as amnesiacs. I assumed Buzz was one of those friends, an old army pal who had simply fallen away when the wife, the son, the job took over Holland's adult life. I had seen enough of Holland's lost pals to assume that, for both these men, the friendship was taken up as cheerfully as it was dropped.

Mr. Charles "Buzz" Drumer was in the corset business, among many more lucrative concerns. He supplied corsets, corselettes, and girdles wholesale to department stores; an old-fashioned profession even in its time, but if anything, I think, it gave him the enviable glow of a womanizer, along with his good looks and his unpadded shoulders. He knew our secrets. He could tell which women wore a grandmotherly boned nylon corset, and which wore the very last gasp (so to speak) of the nineteenth century: the belt-like perforated Waist-in. He took a private pleasure in recognizing the first evidence of circular-stitched bras (within months we all had these rocket boobs), or noting a woman's wiggle which meant she longed to strip off her skirt and adjust her chafing corselette, or—best of all—seeing a shapely woman walk into a room and knowing at a glance that under her dress she wore nothing at all. It was as though he could see us naked.

His proudest invention: naming a new girdle "Persuade" and including with each purchase a booklet on Helena Rubenstein's ten-day reducing diet. A hint of seduction, a promise of hope. I loved how he understood women.

After his first few visits, Buzz came by regularly. His presence gave our house a renewed grace and humor; I liked the idea that neighbors would see him come and go, and would admire the careful way he dressed and his habit, bred in every good Virginia boy, of removing his hat the moment I opened the door, as if I were Mrs. Eleanor Roosevelt herself. And of course I enjoyed his company, as the lonely wife of any missionary appreciates a guest to her far-flung outpost.

One night I'd cooked a steaming lamb pie with peas and recalled there was a contest in the paper about the dish. "If you can name it, you can live free for a year on their dollar! How about that?" I smiled at my son, who stared suspiciously at the vegetables.

Buzz thanked me as I served him and asked what they meant by live free for a year.

"Two thousand dollars?" Holland guessed, winking at me with a smile.

I rapped my husband's hand with a spatula. "Shows what you know about home expenses. *Three* thousand dollars is the prize." I cut a little slice for Sonny, trying not to give him too many peas.

"Seems like you deserve more," Buzz said.

"I'd enter, too, if I could think of a thing to call it," I said.

Holland laughed and said I did live free all year; only it was on his dollar and not the piecrust company's.

Sonny stared at his plate in despair.

We joked about names for it—Shepherdess Pie, Mutton Mutton Who's Got the Mutton?—when my little boy sat up and asked Buzz: "Where your pinkie finger go?"

"Sonny—" I started.

He looked up, helpless. "He got no pinkie finger, Mama."

"It's all right," Buzz said, wiping his mouth and looking very seriously at my son. "It's good to ask questions. I lost it in the war."

"Where you lost it? Alannic or Pacific?" Sonny asked, and we all laughed, because he couldn't possibly have known what he was saying. It was a common question in those days; he must have heard it somewhere. He looked around, smiling as if he'd planned to amuse us.

"Now that's enough," I said. "Eat your pie."

"Bo Peep Pie," Holland added, seriously. "It's worth three thousand dollars."

Sonny looked at his plate and then, perhaps to forestall tasting it, looked at all of us. "Daddy was in the Pacific," he announced.

"Buzz knows that," I said.

I watched my husband very carefully. We'd reached the topic he always preferred not to discuss, but he cut into his pie and said, "We weren't in the war together, you know. Buzz was CO."

Buzz nodded.

"Now were you?" I said, astonished that Holland had just revealed such a startling piece of information.

"The Pacific Ocean," my son murmured to his peas.

Conscientious objectors. "Conchies" was what we called them in Kentucky. A subject of shame, a taboo topic for dinner conversation. There had been a universal consensus in those days, when the country was girded up for war, that it was a disgrace to have men like this. Shirkers, cowards. It was as if a man walked to the altar and said, no, I'm not going to marry this woman after all. It was an extraordinary thing for a young man to be, a bizarre friend for my soldier husband to have made. I could not get my head around it. But war was, as we all knew, a time of secrets.

Buzz blushed at this confession. He began to make less sense to me, not more. How had he lost a finger if he never went to battle? Buzz looked me directly in the eye and said, "It was a hard time," but I felt as if he were trying to tell me something else.

"This pea looking at me," Sonny said, and I told him to push it to the side.

"You'll eat that pea," Holland pronounced.

"So how'd y'all meet? If you never went to war?" I asked Buzz.

"At the hospital, Pearlie," Holland said and took a drink from his beer. He meant the hospital where he himself had gone after his ship went down in the Pacific.

Buzz added: "There was a screwup, and we were roommates."

"It was a screwup for sure. I never had a worse roommate," Holland said.

"I was very neat. And didn't taunt the nurses, like some."

"Not me!"

I took up the spatula and gave them each another slice, noticing that Sonny had only managed to mangle his. I sat back down. After a moment of silence I said, "But I don't understand."

"What, honey?" Holland asked.

"Why would a CO be in a military hospital?"

A pea rolled past the salt and off the table. My son said, "Uh-oh."

Holland was about to answer when Buzz put down his fork and said, "COs were under military control. We were put in a military camp, up north." As he said "up north," he gestured out beyond the house. "And I was sent to that hospital because I was Section Eight."

"Section Eight?"

"Yes," he said. "I went a little crazy."

I looked over at Holland; his eyes avoided mine. It seemed impossible to be discussing all of this so casually.

"Bo Peep Pie!" Sonny shouted, smashing the peas on his plate, ignoring all this talk of war.

I sat quietly, helping Sonny eat his meal. I hadn't ever asked my husband what he had been treated for, or what ward he had been placed in; I knew his ship had gone down and I pictured him recovering from the oil fire and the salt water. But Section Eight was a mental deferral, and those two men were in the same room, the same ward. What had that ocean done to him? I couldn't bring myself to ask any more; the war was something everybody wanted to forget, and the loving nurse in me wanted to protect Holland and his story; wanted to pack it all in cotton wool so we could have peace. So instead I passed around the beer.

That was how we spent those nights: at dinner, with beer and old stories that cleared up nothing. I got the idea to bake a cake for the boys and Buzz exclaimed over it so much that it became a tradition, and we all laughed at the ridiculousness of it. The three of us who had grown up in the Depression with no cakes, and got through a war with no butter, and here we were: a cake every night. And playing fetch with Lyle, Sonny screaming with delight. It was a time of harmless fun, and we were still young enough to enjoy it.

On Saturdays, when Holland worked overtime, Buzz sometimes came early. I didn't mind. He looked after Sonny while I did my chores; it was good to have someone other than the aunts to entertain my son. But there was also something uncomfortable about those times. Buzz would be in the middle of telling me a story, the most banal kind of story, in his bumblebee accent, when he would pause and I'd just know somehow, even with my back turned, that he was staring at me. I swore to myself I would not turn around. It was almost a game.

I wonder what the neighbors thought. I really do. It amused me to imagine they might whisper about Pearlie Cook and her affair with this new visitor.

We were out back on an unusually bright, hot Saturday, pinning clothes to the line and he was handing the damp, bleach-smelling things to me as I fought to hold them firm against the wind. The white sheets cracked in the breeze with the sound of a great fire. That was when Buzz asked if I had a sleeping problem.

"No, it's Holland," I said.

"Poor man."

Holland and I kept two bedrooms, connected by a little hallway. Lyle slept in my room on a sheepskin. Holland slept alone. My husband was a delicate sleeper, as he was delicate in all things, and it had long ago been decided that he'd have his own room. I was the one who insisted on it. To keep his heart safe.

"Had it ever since the war, he can't fall asleep if there's any sound at all. Dogs in the yard at night, that's the worst. And anybody else in the room. Even so, he doesn't sleep most nights."

Buzz kept wringing out clothes and holding them for me to pin.

"I suppose he slept in the hospital," I said.

"We all had different pills to take," he said, smiling.

"And you started up your business."

"Well, took over my father's company," Buzz answered. "Holland was my right-hand man. Then I traveled. Quite a bit, in fact. You have to stockpile a few beautiful vistas in your memory, Pearlie. In case we're rationed again." He glanced at me meaningfully.

I put two of the wooden pins in my mouth, and talking through them, I asked: "Did y'all have a falling out?"

He said nothing for a while. Finally, he said, "Well, I got this nose."

I nodded. "It's a beauty."

"Thank you."

"How did you get it?"

"Holland."

The sun flashed across the billowing sheets. I blinked, turned toward Buzz, and saw him raising a hand to his face just as the sunlight stained him white all along his arm.

"Holland hit you?"

Buzz just cocked his head and watched me. Holland never raised his voice except at the radio, never hit a thing except the couch pillows before he sat down, grinning, with his cigarette. But once, of course, he'd been a different man, a man trained to shoot other men during the war, who drank, who sang with soldiers and hit a friend across the nose.

At last I asked, "Was it over a woman?"

He handed me a pair of trousers. "Yes."

I pulled out the trouser dryer and began to stretch the pants onto it. "Tell me."

"Pearlie," he said. "We were born at a bad time."

"I don't know what you mean. It's a fine time."

I didn't know what he meant by "we." I couldn't imagine what might bind me together with a man like Buzz, as likable as he was. I couldn't draw any kind of line around the two of us.

"You're proud of your house. You have a nice touch."

"It belongs to Holland's family."

"It can't be cheap," he said to me. "I mean Sonny being sick and all."

"Holland's aunts help out. With the bills, the braces, it is a lot. It keeps me inside a good deal, I tell you, taking care of him," I said without thinking. "Of course it's no trouble," I added hastily.

"Now what would you do if you had all the money you needed?"

I had no answer to that. It was a thoughtless question to ask a poor woman with a sick son, something only a rich man would ask. Like wondering aloud to a freshly brokenhearted girl: "What if it turns out he loved you after all?" It was something I had never allowed myself to think about. What would I have done? I'd have moved my family away from a house like that, with glaring neighbors, and stains on the basement walls from the ocean creeping in, with crickets sifting in under the doorsills with the sand . . . to Egypt, to Mali, to some fantasy destination I only knew from books. My God, I'd have flown to Mars with Holland and Sonny and never come back. That was the only answer I could think of. A woman like me, I couldn't afford to name my real desires. I couldn't even afford to know them.

All I said was, "I've *got* everything I need. I'm happy."

"I know, but just imagine . . . where would you live?"

"This house is better than anything my parents had."

"But just say . . . an apartment high above a city? A cliff over an ocean, with a view from your bed? Five hundred acres with a fence all around?"

"What would I do with five hundred acres?" I said without thinking.

Then he looked right at me, not a shy man at all, and I think for a moment I understood.

I stood there, staring at him, with the metal dryer contraption in my hand and the damp trousers over my arm. The sun came in full and lit the world from top to bottom; you could almost hear the jasmine reaching up for it. Then we heard the sound of Holland's car returning and Buzz turned away.

In a moment, Holland shouted "Hey there!" from the house. I heard a bicycle bell, and Sonny heading down the hall in pursuit of love.

And Buzz said nothing else, touching his nose as if touching the memory of pain. He was half to the sun, and the shadow of his ruined hand fell across his long face in the form of another, younger hand cradling his cheek. The wind burrowed into his hair like a living creature. I didn't say a word to him as he went inside, just continued stretching the trousers in the sun to dry. And down I went—into the green deep, flecked with gold and draped with waving plants, endless, bottomless—and forgot what I had glimpsed. I was a careful woman, a good gardener, and I pruned away the doubt.

But you know the heart: every night, it grows a thorn.

It happened when Holland left town. He was a traveling inspector for a fittings company, his area covering all of Northern California, and sometimes he had to stay the night in Redding or Yreka, by the misty sea or the misty mountains, in hotels named the Thunderbird or the Wigwam (like miniature Americas: garishly neon outside, prim and puritan inside). Of course he didn't call; long distance in those days was only used when someone had died, or when you decided to tell someone, too late, that you loved them after all. My neighbor Edith Furstenberg had come to visit before supper, wearing her new aqua seven-way blouse from Macy's—"Only three ways, really, if you think about it"; she wanted to gossip about the Sheng family who had been excluded from Southwood by community vote and how ashamed she was of our town, how ashamed after all the Chinese had suffered.

"It's hard for the colored, too," I said.

"But not here in San Francisco. Not here in the Sunset, thank God."

We tried out her blouse in all seven ways, none of them appealing. "Don't ever change!" she shouted at me, in that fashionable phrase, from some television show I'd never seen. I washed some delicates in something she'd loaned me called Re-Clean ("so safe you can smoke while using it"). Then Sonny and I were left alone with *Sky King* on the radio, and for half an hour my son stared into the carved-wood lyre of its mouth, surely understanding nothing but that he loved it. He fell asleep in my lap and I put him to bed.

It had been an unseasonably hot day, followed by a humid night. Just before sunset, it had briefly rained, and the last of the warm sun turned the air to steam that shimmered down to the ocean. The German and Irish families were out grilling, walking the streets, standing at corners and laughing as the men threw cans of beer to one another and the children wrestled in the still-wet grass. It was so delightfully warm that I opened the drapes and windows, but, unsettled by the idea of neighbors peering in, I turned out all the lights and sat in the kitchen, satisfied: water in the kettle, Lyle at my feet.

The singing kettle filled the air with noise for some time before I reached it. The stove's red eye was all that lit the room. I took the kettle off the flame, and as it calmed and fell to silence, I heard the knocking that must have begun while the kettle was sounding its alarm. A tapping at the windowpane. I turned and I was reminded of an image that always haunted me: after the war, I'd heard that Berliners replaced their blown-out window glass with doctors' X-rays—before my eyes adjusted, all I saw was a broad white hand spread on a black windowpane.

"Buzz," I said, unlatching the door.

His eyes looked around the dim kitchen. "When no one answered the front door, I thought you might be having an affair." He laughed. He was in a dark suit and a dark, shiny tie, and when he stepped over the doorsill he removed his hat, as always. And then he said, "Pearlie, what are you doing alone in the dark—"

"Don't," I said quickly, because his hand was reaching for the switch. I found that I'd put my hand on his; it was as smooth as touching a glove. He didn't ask why. He merely stood there, handsome Buzz, with a hat in his hand. He looked like he wanted to sell me something. I laughed, which caused a baffled smile to flicker on his face.

"Is Holland around?"

"He's out of town, and Sonny's sleeping—"

"Oh, of course," he said, shaking his head. "I forgot he's traveling, how stupid of me. And selfish."

"No, no."

"He's up in Yreka, right? So I'm wrecking your night alone." A wry smile.

"Not at all," I said.

"Yreka Bakery," he murmured to himself, smiling.

"What's that?"

"Oh, it's a silly joke. It's a mirror name, you can read it backward and forward. I wonder if there really is a bakery there. If there isn't, we should start one."

I laughed. "I never heard of that! I have to tell Holland."

"Too hot to hoot," he said. "That's another."

I said that was a good one.

"Oh, it's foolishness from my childhood."

Once again, we were alone in my silent house.

"You came all this way," I said at last. "Want some tea? Or no, maybe a whiskey. I feel like a whiskey, don't you?"

"I could hardly turn one down," he said with a kind of relief. I poured out two glasses and we both downed them in a second; that was how you did it in those days. I poured us another round and went to the freezer to get the ice. Lyle jumped around beneath me, hoping to get a piece; for some unknown reason, his silence came with a love of chewing ice.

"What a strange, warm night," I said.

"Ain't it?"

"Too hot to hoot!"

I opened the freezer (a lion's roar) and pulled out the ice trays, sliding the little metal levers and releasing the ice into a bucket. I threw one into the air and Lyle caught it like a dolphin. Loudly, he began to crack the cold little thing with delight.

He said, "The streetcar had all its windows steamed up, it was like a greenhouse. You know they're growing orchids in them now, right by the door."

I laughed. "How practical."

"And Venus flytraps. For ones who don't pay fares."

"Here's to spring in San Francisco. You never know."

I toasted him and again we drank.

"Holland tells me you still live in a bachelor apartment with one burner on the stove. Why don't you move somewhere better?"

"So I could cook for myself instead of coming over here?"

"Well, I—"

"I went away traveling, I left it empty for a few years. Never got to improve it. Lived in worse in Istanbul, they still read by kerosene there. And I have a sentimental attachment to that burner, I'll have you know."

"Any family around?"

He looked into his drink as if the answer were at the bottom. "No, there's nobody around. My father died last year."

"I'm sorry to hear that."

"And my mother has been gone a long time now," he said, smiling sadly and taking another sip. "I was surprised to have to take over the business out here. It wasn't something I'd ever planned on. I'm not the business type."

"What had you planned on?"

A shrug, a nervous look at the door. "That's what I had traveled to discover."

"Did you discover it?"

He nodded. We downed our drinks again. I reached for my cigarettes and he put his hand on mine. Neither of us moved.

"Pearlie?"

He was so different. After two or three bolts of whiskey, he'd stopped playing the affable golden boy. He seemed a thousand years old, with the lights from the houses cutting him clean in half and deepening the sun lines on his face. The darkness drained everything of color, and so his bright blond hair had gone stark white. With his hand on mine, I could feel his heart racing.

"I hope you can help me," he said, just as he had the day he'd first shown up at my door. Yet this time, he spoke in a kind of whisper I had never heard before. He moved his hand to my arm.

I was afraid of what he was going to say. "Buzz, it's late."

He tried to interrupt me but now I was setting down the ice bucket, throwing another chunk of ice to my hysterical dog, chattering: "Holland will be back tomorrow, you better run if you want to catch the streetcar—"

He said he knew Holland would be back tomorrow, and that was the point. He had not come to see Holland. He had come that night to talk to me.

I didn't know what was happening; I didn't know what I wanted to happen. His touch suddenly felt very warm on my arm.

"Listen to me," he said, "I have to tell you something."

"Buzz, I think—"

But his voice stopped me, and his hand moved to my shoulder:

"Pearlie, listen to me. Please listen to me."

Something in me shifted; it was as if an alarm had sounded. Here was a plain, pale face stained with longing, and in that darkness he looked nothing like the man I had known for weeks, the confident old friend. I stood quiet and still, pressed against the wall.

And then he told me. With a soft country voice and his eyes gazing at a photograph on the wall. A careful man, touching my arm. I think he had never talked of love before. For you see he had not come all that way on the streetcar that night for Holland; he had come for me, Pearlie Cook. He had pieced that speech together over the years, practiced it over and over in his bachelor's rooms downtown: a prisoner building a palace out of toothpicks; carefully, slowly, he gave me a masterpiece only a lonely man can make.

And when he was done, he let go of my arm. He took a step away from me, back into the shadow. I could hear Lyle cracking his ice like a nut. A tinker on his way back from his rounds broke out in song: "Grind your scissors! Grind your knives!" I stood with my cheek flat against the wall, looking out at our neighborhood and the shapes I knew so well, the light-rimmed borders of my world.

"You're lying," I said. "He's just sickly. It's his heart."

Buzz said he wasn't lying. His hand reached out again for my arm, but I flinched away.

"Don't touch me," I said, though I was barely able to breathe.

Then he told me something very true: "It's time for you to think, Pearlie."

He had not used the word "lovers." No, Buzz said "together"— that he and Holland had been "together" for a long time before I reappeared. They were "together" in the hospital during the war, minds bound with gauze in the dayroom, sharing the view out on the ocean; "together" living on Buzz's money and taking tentative steps in the new world. The one that had broken them, hateful of conchies and cowards and everyone who wasn't square and true as a crossbeam; they had survived it "together." A crooked romance, in that room with one burner. A love story. Until, one day, Holland got up from bed and said he was going to be married. A fight; a broken nose; shouts from a high window to a man running down the street. Without even knowing it, I had taken this man's lover away and hidden him, safe from the world, in my vine-covered house. Now he had found him. He had come to me, to my front door, to break the curse I had not even known was on my life. He said it as if it were a beautiful thing. In his mind I'm sure it was.

"You must have known, Pearlie. A smart woman like you always knows."

We heard the sound of a family walking by, their dog barking at the scent of Lyle inside, their children babbling meaninglessly and the adults laughing beyond my walls.

"I didn't know, not precisely, I knew something was—"

"I can only say I'm sorry."

"Is that why you came here?" I asked in a sudden rage. "Showed up at our door and . . . and sneaked into my life? Lord, my son's life—"

"I know you don't believe it yet, but we're on the same side."

"Don't you—"

"We were born at a bad time," he told me. "We made the choices we had to make. They were hard enough choices, and it was nice to think it all was over. But now there's another one to be made."

The alarm I felt was not just the shock of his words, as startling as someone jerking back the curtain in a dark room, blinding me with painful sunlight. It was that I had not known my husband at all. We think we know the ones we love, and though we should not be surprised to find that we don't, it is heartbreak nonetheless. It is the hardest kind of knowledge, not just about another but about ourselves. To see our lives as a fiction we have written and believed. Silence and lies. The sensation I felt that evening—that I did not know my Holland, did not know myself, that it was perhaps impossible to know a single soul on earth—it was a fearful loneliness.

"I'm so sorry. I didn't want to hurt you."

"Stop it. Stop it, stop saying that." I felt naked and ashamed. It was as if every new revelation, every fresh thought in my head, were like a scalpel, revealing things that should not ever be seen. What about his fragile transposed heart? Another fiction of mine, another lie to keep my life serene.

And yet—beneath all the jolts of surprise and grief, I could feel a small, growing surge of relief. He made sense, my husband, at last. The storm-cloud expressions, and separate bedrooms, and "illness" as his aunts had put it; the inconsistencies that I had blamed myself for, the imperfect wife, my own failure to save him. At least I was not insane. For here it was: what I had prepared myself for. I had known his allure; I'd seen the longing in others' eyes. I had always thought it would be another woman. That was the usual way of things. Here was the awful thing, unexpectedly: a man.

It was more than two years, apparently. That was what Buzz told me that evening. My mind scrambled to catch hold of it all—years together, years of a romance I did not want to imagine, and, not long after Holland came to pick me up at the boardinghouse, a scene when he told Buzz to go to hell and never come back. A broken nose, a shout from a high window. A whisper in my ear: "I need you to marry me." He might have said: "I need you to hide me." Like a protected witness, a life in our little house, calm as can be: a boy, a wife, a barkless dog. Some love in there, for all of us. Some happiness for him. But the old love story was not yet over.

I could feel Lyle jumping against my dress, begging for more. "Pearlie."

"What do you want from me?" I asked.

"I need your help." From the bucket came a sigh, the melting ice collapsing on itself. "I'm leaving soon. I'm going to travel again, and I am taking Holland with me."

I said that was not going to happen.

"Yes, it will, Pearlie. You know you can't keep living this way."

"Let us be," I said. "Why did you come here?"

"To talk to you. To set you free."

"Damn you. Don't pretend you're helping me—"

"We have to help each other."

"What does Holland say?"

Buzz didn't move. Headlights of a car going by lit up his hair, shining like a cap of silver cloth; he was handsome again in that light, terribly in love, heartbroken, a jilted lover trying to hold back any sign of it from me.

"I see," I said.

"Yes. It's complicated."

"Holland doesn't want to leave us, does he?"

"There is something holding him back—" he began.

I shook my head to keep from hearing him. Holland and I had talked about our friends and our childhoods and movies and books and politics—we had agreed and disagreed and had our fights and merry moments over a beer—but I think it's fair to say we had never spoken honestly in all our lives. And, in my peculiar way, I had thought that I was happy. At the time, my sense was that marriage was like a hotel shower: you get the temperature right and someone just beyond the wall turns on his shower and you are stung with ice water, you adjust the heat only to hear him yelp from pain, he adjusts his, and so on until you reach a tepid compromise that both of you can endure.

"Let us be. I can't help you."

"I know you will. You must."

"But he's my husband, I love him."

"Now you know you're not the only one," he said. It was a different voice, not the one he'd practiced over the years. The fractured voice of a man who traveled the world to escape a broken heart, who returned to an empty apartment, with all the old photos, nothing changed. Who lay awake wondering how he lost all he ever cherished.

Not the only one. As if all claims were equal claims, and marriage and children and years of life meant nothing; as if his love were as dense and bright as a star, outweighing any others. Mine, my son's. The world went not to the meek but to the heart-wrung, the starving, the passionate. The rest barely counted as living. The world went to men like Buzz.

It had been a long time since I'd seen straight through a man. I had spent my days caring for my little boy, and for my husband, and for my house; it was simpler not to notice other people. Other people hide themselves, after all; they work so hard to do it. But a writer once said that pain reveals things. I think that was true of Buzz, when the light came in and I glimpsed the suffering that had brought him to this.

I watched a car's headlights reach through the window and draw a line across the poor man's broken nose. It stilled me, and for a moment I believed him. There was the proof of the suffering he was willing to endure. There it was, smashed into his face so he could never for an instant forget it.

"You won't be abandoned, I promise you that. I've thought it all over."

"I'm sure you have."

"I can take care of you, Pearlie," he told me.

I threw Lyle more ice and he caught it, taking it out into the hall where he could fracture it in privacy. "I can't listen to this."

"I can help you if you help me."

He said it very plainly then. For a long time, in that living room, he explained what he had in mind, and I said nothing at all as he described how he would give me his fortune if I would help him. You could say he was bargaining for my husband. "I can take care of you. Think of Sonny, and sending him to college. Life isn't set, life isn't done. Think of what you want."

I said he couldn't be serious, and he said nothing.

"Help you how?" I took him by the arm but couldn't look at his face. Instead my eyes searched the room, that old living room of mine, that old witness to the events of my life. The wind blew around the house, and there, through the bottom of the door, a little sand began to make its way in. Off somewhere, a car radio started playing "Kiss of Fire."

"There is someone in the way," he said, smiling a little.

I would have lived in the Outside Lands forever, clipping my newspaper by the ocean, vines creeping over the house as in a fairy tale—Sleeping Duty—aunts numbing me from time to time with gifts and stories, kissing my husband every night before I went to bed; I would have borne it. But he came to my house, like a wave at high tide, and ruined the little castle I had built. I could not believe what I was hearing; I knew it was bad for all of us, and what he told me felt like an unearned punishment. Like an electrocution.

"Don't ever come back here," I said.

After he left, I closed and locked the door, then every window in the house, as if somehow he'd break in during the night and I'd awaken and find him standing in my living room. "Think about it, please call me," he said at the door before I closed it on him, "EX-brook 2-8600." I can still remember the exchange. I sat on the couch with Lyle beside me. Together, we watched the bars of light that moved along the floor as one car after another made its way down our quiet street. We listened to the neighbors calling to one another from house to house, talking about the Rosenberg or the Sheng cases, the conversation drifting until they said good night. After long periods of silence, we could hear the growl of the Pacific. Lyle did not move from my side. My husband did not call. And Buzz did not return.

I drank the rest of the whiskey—half a bottle at least—and then, after the streets were cleared and the cool of the ocean took over the night again, after I went to look at Sonny sleeping with one leg thrown out over the covers, eyelashes matted from a passing nightmare, mouth slightly open like a girl waiting for a kiss, I drunkenly stumbled into my bedroom, weeping, and caught sight of the wastepaper basket.

There, in a mound, lay the clippings: the news I had censored for the sake of Holland's transposed heart. A heart, it turned out, that beat as regularly as my own. A catalog of American daily life that the rest of us had lived through and my husband had not. I turned the basket over on the bed and made a leaf pile of paper. One by one, I read them and thought of the countless other stories I had clipped throughout our marriage. I was drunk and stunned and wild with revelations, my heart muscling its way through my chest like a panicked man in a crowded room.

1953. It was a world with a war that had just ended and, like a devil that grows a new tail after you've chopped one off, another war had begun. With a draft and an enemy just like the one before, only this time there were nuclear weapons; there were veterans' cemeteries that refused to bury Negro soldiers; there was a government telling you what to look for in a nuclear flash, what kind of structure to hide under should the sirens start wailing—though they must have known that it would have been madness to look or hide or consider anything except lying down and taking your death in with one full breath. There were the subcommittee hearings with Sheedy asking McLain on TV, "Are you a red?" whereupon McLain threw water into his face, and Sheedy threw water back and knocked off his glasses. A world in which TV stations were asked to segregate characters on their shows for Southern viewers, in which all nudes were withdrawn from a San Francisco art show because "local mother Mrs. Hutchins's sensibilities are shaken to the core"; and beautiful Angel Island became a guided missile station, and a white college student was expelled for proposing to a Negro, and they were rioting against us in Trieste; the Allies freed Trieste not many years ago, and suddenly they hated us . . . and hovering above all this, every day in the paper, that newsprint visage like the snapshot of a bland Prometheus: Ethel Rosenberg's face.

When would the all clear come? Didn't somebody promise us an all clear if we were good, and clean, and nice, and were willing to die for things, and believe in things, and agreed to do everything right? Where was our all clear?

But there was more. An invisible world, now made obvious, like those codes that can only be read with special glasses; it had been there all along: a list of men arrested for sex crimes, a quarter of them for congress with other men, their names right there in the paper; following a directive to "break the back" of an imagined security issue—barely reported, certainly uncriticized—the hundreds of State Department firings for rumors of deviant desire. The white navy doctor set free from his trial for gouging out the eyes of a Negro man who suggested "a vile perverted act." And young Norman Wong smiling in a neat black suit, saddled with a $14,000 mortgage on his fruit ranch, who coaxed a white air force captain—his lover—to murder his wife for the insurance money, saying, "I loved her too much to shoot her myself." That photo of plain Silvia Wong—the unkillable wife—in a blouse buttoned to the top to hide the wounds, weeping at the courthouse because she still loved Norman and if he went to jail she would have to wait two years to bear his children.

Later I would face my worst fears in the library, forcing myself to read about acts even the court stenographer found too "repulsive" to be included. Police peering through windows and keyholes, drilling holes in walls, building a false ceiling so they could lie in the rafters and spy on poor unsuspecting men. The maximum sentence for those crimes, I would discover, had just been raised to life in prison. If not prison, then registration as a sex offender; my son's home would always be recorded in red ink. And I would come across a more chilling alternative: sterilization. Unable to discover whether "perverts" had been exempted by 1953, I would find an astounding figure: the number of California men degraded in this way. Twenty thousand. I would leave those books as I found them: dog-eared, smudging, foxed and torn, worn away by desperate readers who had come before me.

That night, in my deranged state, those newspaper clippings stood before me like criminals in a lineup, staring out with bleary eyes, each one an aspect of the world that Buzz revealed to me. All the silence and lies of a nation. Holland's heart would have to bear it now. Like a king's taster who has eaten his limit of poison, I could not take it anymore—all I'd tried to hide from him—I could not swallow any more of the world.

I pulled out the gloves Buzz had given me; I put them on. The red bird fluttered in my palm. I clenched it tight inside my fist; I felt its awful twitching struggle.

The telephone operator greeted me kindly and I told her to dial EXbrook 2-8600. A crickety voice answered. I asked to be put through to Mr. Drumer, please, and she said, Gal you can't be calling this early. I said someone's life was at stake, and that seemed to get her. A pop of sound and a man was on the line, sleeptalking, saying Pearlie? Pearlie?

"I have to protect my son," I said.

He wanted to know if I would help him. "That's what I'm telling you." I sat there staring at the dawn as he said what he wanted me to do. From the front door came the shivering sound of bottles on the step. A truck started up and rolled away. All I could do was sit there on the phone bench and listen, shaking a little, thinking everyone must be an optical illusion, even the one we love. We think we know them, flat and simple—not at all.

They are faceted in ingenious ways, with hundreds of hidden sides, impossible to discover even in a lifetime. Razor-sharp, frightening sides. I heard the man talking softly in my ear. I could save my son, if not my marriage. Life could be exchanged; could be better, what you'd dreamed of; could be built on a cliff above the roaring world. A choice: take this, or nothing. There was no other option, in those days long ago, in my outpost by the sea. Not for colored girls like me.

II

J will never forget Eslanda Goode Robeson, wife of the singer Paul Robeson, called before the committee that year. Cohn and McCarthy questioned her about being a Communist, and that proud colored woman sat in her flowered dress and hat and declined to answer, under protection of the Fifth and Fifteenth amendments. The Fifteenth? asked a flustered Roy Cohn. "Yes, the Fifteenth," Mrs. Robeson told him regally. "I am Negro, you know. I have been brought up to seek protection under the Fifteenth Amendment as a Negro." Cohn told her it was nonsense; the Fifteenth was about the right to vote. But she shook her head: "I have always sought protection under it . . . you see, I am a second-class citizen in this country and, therefore, feel the need of the Fifteenth. That is the reason I use it. I am not quite equal to the rest of the white people." Cohn could get nowhere else with her; it was beyond translation, her version of life in our country.

They don't teach Eslanda Goode Robeson in schools. There is no room in textbooks, among all the myriad battles and treaties, for history's wives. But what she said about needing extra armor to protect herself, I never forgot it. It glowed in my mind. It guided my life like a sextant.

We were the only Negro family in the Sunset. It would have made a difference if I'd had a friend to trust, some colored woman who could hide me and Sonny in her sewing room the way she might hide a beaten wife; I might have fled into her arms. But I was not beaten; I was, in my way, beloved. And I had no friend like that. Even Edith, the only Jew in our neighborhood, mirroring my solitude across the street, was not someone I could turn to. There was no question of fleeing that night with Sonny; imagine a colored woman walking down the highway with her crippled boy, seeking aid from other migrants. That was no way to save him. The logical place to turn would have been the Negro community on Fillmore, but we had cut ourselves off from that world as well.

At the time, I blamed his aunts. They claimed to have come from Hawaii, descended on their father's side from a West Indian sea captain's daughter and a grandson of Captain Cook, and that lovely but improbable legend allowed them to feel distinct. They were typical of the old Negro society in San Francisco: cultured, intellectual, eager to set up the right kind of marriage, the men going around with walking sticks and the women with cameo brooches of Caucasian faces. They considered themselves apart from the rest of their race, as did Holland. I remember one time, one of the first dinners I made for the aunts, when they told me: "We may have had an African ancestor four or five generations ago, but as you can see the European blood has diluted it." I listened to that speech with wonder, almost admiration. What an attractive fantasy: to believe you could leave race problems behind.

Yet they clung to segregation. "We prefer it this way," they told me and Holland. "Negroes should work, eat, and shop together." They had wanted to sell off the "Sunset property" as they called it and have me and Holland move close to them on Fillmore, in the Negro district, where it was growing crowded with families who could find no other place that would rent to them, but I put my foot down. I wanted a different life, a better one, in my mind. And so we lived out by the ocean, far from our people. It might not have been the right thing to do, in the end; it could be I was trying to pass as much as the aunts, as much as Holland himself. But I remember Thurgood Marshall came to San Francisco that very spring of 1953, and the paper quoted him as saying that the reason some Negroes favored segregated armies was so they could be generals. Perhaps the aunts favored a segregated San Francisco so they could be mayors of that little world. They did not see what was happening, what was about to happen in our country. Poor old women; I think they were too terrified.

Of course, I was just as much to blame. I was as terrified as anyone, knowing the danger my husband was in. Had he not seen the recent photo from Compton, a day's drive from us: a burning cross in the yard of a Negro running for Senate? Or had I clipped that from the paper, as well? What a tragic time to be a man like him.

I did not know how to fight a white man; I was born without that muscle. But I knew one thing: I knew silence, which like an exotic poison—odorless, tasteless—brings a subtle madness to the victim. I became half mad with fear and shame, now that my carefully constructed world had been tornado-torn from its foundations, the walls and windows hurled at me so that all I could do was crouch and wait for it to subside. My doubts, my questions; I stoppered them like moths in a killing jar. Some tinge of wifely duty still colored my actions, hoping to protect Holland and his past. Buzz had made everything plain to me, but I still went about my day to the syncopated beating of a transposed heart, and my instincts were those of a nurse who discovers, late in her rounds, that her patients have fled in the night. Whose life shall she save now? Her own?

I found myself unable to sleep, remembering how chance had brought us together—twice—and considering, like a woman about to pawn an heirloom, exactly what it could get me, what it was worth, what I was preparing to forsake. Not just our marriage but what we had done to get there, that secret story. Our love story, you might say. It was a simple tale from the war, but it was not the version I ever told to strangers or friends. I kept it hidden. I thought we had left that behind us, beneath us, yet here it showed itself, nightly, surfacing like a body from the deep.

It was the summer of 1943; we were still in our teens. One afternoon, Holland's mother delivered his draft card to him on the front porch where we sat listening to the radio. "Well look at that," he said. He was a quiet boy; you could not make out what he thought of death. It could have been a stranger to him, or terrified him to the core, but his mother, a tough skinny widow, was well acquainted. She stated clearly: "Now son, don't you sign it. This ain't our war. I won't lose you." Holland looked up at me with his square, beautiful face and took a sip from his tea and then we could hear it: the ice clinking in his shaking hand. Poor frightened young men, being called off to battle. Like townspeople watching a cyclone headed toward them, you could feel it coming: the end of youth.

"What do you think, Pearlie?" he asked me. He dabbed a handkerchief across his forehead, which had darkened in the summer sun. Drops of sweat shone in his hair.

Holland, do you remember my shocked silence? How I sat there in the rocking chair and said nothing? A bee was trapped in a lantern, buzzing like a bank alarm. We rocked back and forth to the radio, which was playing "Good As I Been to You," of all sad things. I finally got up the nerve to look over at you. Your beautiful face, your frightened hand. I knew what I wanted, but I had no idea if I had a right to want it, and I had no way of saying: Don't go, I need you. What was my life without you? All I said was "Oh!" You stared at me and seemed to understand, and it was all we ever spoke about the matter.

Holland chose—as men often have the luxury of choosing—to do nothing. His registration deadline came and went and the brown paper, stabbed with a rusted thumbtack above his bed, grew blond in the sun. His mother, knowing what it meant to let time pass, came into Holland's room one morning and, after pulling down the shade, ripped the registration form off the thumbtack. As she walked back out of the dimmed room, Holland sat up and asked what she was doing. "I'm throwing it away," she said.

"But I was going to send it in," he told her.

She stood in the hallway, wiping her hands on her flowered Hoover apron. She was a farmer's widow, used to saving what the world tried to take away. "You can't send it in," she said.

"I'm going to."

"I already told the neighbors you left this Monday. Keep that shade down, and stay upstairs, you hear me? I've made up my mind, it's done." Without another word she went downstairs and he was left in his bedroom, darkened except for a shaft of light coming through a hole in the shade, dustily illuminating a pack of cards. Holland stared at the shade for a moment. And then he closed the door.

How did you survive it? Your world was as cramped as a sailor's: just a sunless bedroom, a chamber pot, and the three feet of hallway that could not be seen from the road. You were forbidden to go outside at all, to stand at the window, or sing, or bounce a ball against the wall—forbidden, in other words, to be a boy. You were a monk, with your silence and the books I brought you, sequestered from the dangers of the outside world. How did you not break into pieces, knowing that if a neighbor caught sight of you, by nightfall the whole town would be there with yellow paint to pour over you and pots to bang in a fury at a slacker like you, a Negro coward? I know you studied every battle of that war, every ship of colored soldiers headed out across the Pacific and blown to smithereens. You kept track of figures and death tolls as any other boy would follow baseball statistics, and I know it was to touch the real world now and then, to have it hurt you, to feel alive. You lived behind the looking glass, in the hollow of a tree, in the deathless world women had made for you.

I visited that prison, wallpapered with newsprint. I arrived a few times a week with sheet music in my hand. His mother would sit downstairs alone, playing the bad piano I was meant to be learning—"Rock of Ages" over and over—while I went up and visited her son. I always brought books hidden in my sheet music; I must have checked out everything in the library. And we would read together, in silence or in whispers, until it was time for me to step back into the strange, bright sunlight of a day you never saw.

I memorized each corner of your room. Of course I did; I was a girl in love. The lariat that hung beside the window like a snake; your metal bed, painted a sanitary white, sagging like a prison cot; the shadowless statue of a horseback Indian; your copper-rivet jacket that I borrowed on cool afternoons. And I memorized your face in that dim light, your smile glowing when I entered. Your muted silhouette as you stood against the pulled shade: broad-shouldered with skinny legs and hair grown out. How you mouthed hello and motioned for me to sit beside you. I committed your room to memory. I told myself it was so that, on thundercloud days, I could navigate the stuffy darkness as in a game of blindman's bluff. Really it was so that later, in my own bed, I could close my eyes and imagine myself beside you in the hushed foxhole that was your world. I loved you like a field on fire.

Did you love me? It was hard not to wonder, lying awake those nights after Buzz Drumer's visit, thinking of those months in your dark room. Love of some kind, I suppose: love of a lion for the tamer, a coin for the pocket. But not what I had hoped. Not, I was terrified to realize, the love you had for that white man.

There was a romance to it, at least. A childish romance warming into an adolescent one, as we sat together day after day; fumblings with books become fumblings with hands. It was the dream of my youth to be locked in a room with you, with handsome Holland Cook, but once it had come true, I did not know what to do. Young people are inept at love; it is like being given a flying machine, and you leap inside, ready to set off as you've always dreamed, yet you don't have the first notion of how to make it start, much less how to move it. That was true of us, in that humid room. Staring at each other as the sunset lit the window shade like a cinema screen, the one rip burning flaming red. It set the tone for our lives together, those days in a warm sealed room, reading books in a whisper, terrified of discovery. Is that what made you marry me, I wondered? Children hiding from our country, that angry father.

We did our war duty, his mother and I. Somehow, on one set of ration stamps, she managed to run the farm without suspicion: she punched up oleo in a bag to make it look like butter, and gathered milkweed pods with the colored ladies' auxiliary (for soldiers' down vests), and I ordered a poster to hang in our window, of a blue house with great red letters: THIS IS A V HOME— WE SALVAGE, CONSERVE, AND REFUSE TO SPREAD RUMORS! We did not merely act the part of citizens in war, all the better to hide our beloved boy. We were good people; we never doubted the need for "mock" apple pie so the boys could have real apples. It was a righteous war. But it was not our war.

Holland, you nodded when we told you colored men were used as cannon fodder; if they were not dispatched on fatal missions, they were sent to mess halls to be blown to bits with the white boys they served. No one should blame you. They might as well blame everyone else who hid, like the men who took up cod fishing because it meant a deferral, or the women who counterfeited rations for a wedding cake; we are all willing to cheat to some extent, and you didn't do it just for butter. Later, you did your part.

If he hadn't taken ill, he might have lasted out the war. I sat by his dark bedside, holding his volcano-hot hand, whispering to him to hold on, hold on—his mother half demented from grief, constantly asking me: "What do we do, Pearlie, what do we do?"— until, just before dawn, I announced we had to fetch the doctor. The decision was all mine. It was not the doctor, though, who told. He was a kind, old-fashioned, whiskey-smelling white man who stopped toothaches with melted rubber and sewed catgut stitches with the precision of his seamstress mother. It was the neighbors who heard him driving to the house that morning and saw a healthy old widow standing on the porch, motioning to help someone inside. Within twenty-four hours the police were there with a draft officer and Holland was pulled, still sweating from sickness, into a waiting Ford while I screamed from the living-room window as if the nerves had been ripped out of me. In my mind, I had killed him.

"Did your mother make you do it, boy?" the draft officer asked. Holland sat in a perfectly square little room with one long window; on its frosted glass, the shadow of a holly tree waved back and forth.

Oh no, Holland told the man without looking at him. Then he pointed out it wasn't something he did; it was just something he neglected to do. His mother had never said a word.

"Was it philosophical beliefs?"

He didn't know, and wondered why he had to put anything.

The man looked up at Holland and a terrible green reptile fury flashed over his features. "Boy, I can't put down that you're just a goddamn Negro coward. I can't have that in my district. It don't mean you're not going to war." Then, after making a few notes on his pad, he added, "I wouldn't come back here, boy."

He was drafted after all, and put on an army bus; his mother could barely look at him to say goodbye; she was so cocooned in grief and shame and the waste of it all. She gave him a kiss and I gave him an old charm that he later lost in the ocean: a tarnished silver feather. I did not know what else to give a boy headed to purgatory. He hung it around his neck and tried to smile as the military bus began to rumble, pulling away from me and our hometown. He never saw Kentucky again or his mother, who died from a bad heart the following spring. He would never have seen me again if blind chance had not led me right by him on the beach. He never wrote in all those years.

And then I was alone. Not only because I had lost Holland,

which seemed like an unclimbable mountain of grief, but because of how things are in a small town. I was as smeared with yellow paint as Mrs. Cook, as much as Holland himself. My own family was ashamed of me, and it was this shame that sent me away from them forever.

It was 1944, and his unit had been at sea only two weeks before they were blown to pieces and Holland found himself naked, his brown skin burning in the oily middle of the Pacific. He floated along on a bamboo chest, a 1-A Ishmael, staring at a sky all green and saffron and cotton wool, treading and waiting. Did it occur to him this was all because a girl back home had tried to save him? A girl who blamed herself for breaking the spell, for deciding to go for the doctor? I wonder what went through his head in those mad hours before they found him. A drowning man, grasping for any hand. Perhaps he never left that sea.

The sun sank, with the ship, into the raisin-colored water. Glowworm lights of rescue boats arrived, echo-yelling in the darkness, and Holland was discovered babbling about a feather; he was taken to a medical boat, then to the overcrowded hospital where he was mistakenly assigned a white roommate who lay asleep for days until one morning, as Holland smoked out on the balcony, the stranger awakened and Holland said, laughing: "The dead have arisen." That was it: the moment. When the love story passed from me to the man in the bed, staring at the vision before him. The moment, like the smallest gear of a hidden machine, that set our lives in motion.

Did you love me? I wondered as I remembered it all over again. I had to go over every image, pick it apart for clues. I had not thought about it, not in years. I had wrapped my story in tissue and put it away. I had never told it to a soul. Not until the day I walked with Buzz along a boardwalk by the sea.

❧

There weren't many places where a white man and a colored girl
could meet in 1953. I could not leave Sonny too long with the
aunts, and Buzz knew only his part of downtown, so on my
suggestion we met by the ocean, at an amusement park called
Playland-by-the-Sea.

It covered the ocean edge of Golden Gate Park, like the fringe
of a scarf, and if you were foolish enough to stand in the chilly Pacific and look back on the city, you would see it laid out before
you against the sky: roller coasters like sentinel dragons flanking
the games of chance and restaurants. Hot House Tamales! Salt
Water Taffy! Chocolate-Dipped Bananas! They lined up like a car-
toon strip, on what would be the finest beach property in America if it wasn't for the fog, so that only a few braved the seawall:
Russians remembering their lost homeland, pairs of secret lovers,
and people, like us, who sought its cloud-cover to hide.

I told him my story, there with the foghorns singing to the
west of us and calliopes singing to the east. And when I was done,
Buzz removed his soft hat so that his gold hair lay shining and
motionless in the wind. How hollow, to have no secrets left; you
shake yourself and nothing rattles. You're boneless as an anem-
one. Children ran by, racing for the fun house, half delighted
and terrified. I watched his face very carefully, but I did not know
him well enough to recognize his moods, a crinkling of his eyes
that might be a sign of anger or of doubt. I tried to see what my
story meant to him. He had always thought of Holland as a war
hero, a beautiful wounded soldier, and I wondered if this story
might warp that image: a flame placed too near a wax statue.

"I don't expect you to understand," I said firmly.

"How did your parents not know?" Buzz asked after a moment of frowning thought. "Going to piano lessons, disappearing
all the time with books. They must have guessed."

"They didn't pay too much attention to me."

He said that was foolish, I was their daughter.

"I wasn't . . ." I began, pulling my coat close around me. "I wasn't quite what he wanted."

"It must have been awful for you," he said, but I could not look at him, so I didn't know which he was talking about, my father or my husband.

"It was worse for Holland. For everyone to see him like that, dragged out of the house."

"I don't know," Buzz said. "I think it might have been worse for you. It's always worse for the one who stays."

We wives are such territorial creatures. Not just where our husbands and sons and houses are concerned, but over the painful past. Like the Chinese soldiers bricked into castle walls to make eternal guardians of their ghosts, we are bound to protect that past, though we are helpless to do anything but moan and shake our chains. This man had come to take away my husband, and what I needed to tell him was that he, too, was wrong; there was another Holland Cook he didn't know. Though Buzz might have returned after years to claim his old lover, he knew him no better than I.

"Why did you tell me that story?" he asked.

"I thought you should hear it."

"It does make sense of things," he said. He was facing me as we walked, head bent down close to mine.

"I gave up my youth in that town to take care of him," I said hotly.

"What I—"

"I gave up any kind of love they had for me, I had to leave. And I lost him."

Buzz said he understood. He looked around; perhaps I was too loud.

"No, you don't," I said in a struggling voice. Buzz put his hand on my arm and the fabric was so thin that I could feel the unsteadiness of his pulse. "I don't think you possibly could. No matter how well you think you know him."

"I don't claim to know him."

"But you said—"

"When I met Holland in the hospital," he said, keeping his hand on my arm, "the Section Eight hospital, the one he never told you about, I'd never seen anyone so beautiful. Or so in pain. He was shell-shocked." That was when he released me and I moved away. "He'd recovered a little by the time I got there, but he was like . . . a plaster cast of a young man, just the outside and nothing within. He was very fragile and quiet and I took care of him. I was hardly able to take care of myself, but he was worse off, I think. It wasn't knowing him that made me fall in love with him."

"He never mentioned me, I guess."

Buzz shook his head. "He talked about Kentucky like it was a million years ago. But I knew who you were."

"But not what I'd given up."

"I didn't know about the war. You're right, I can't possibly understand what it's like now, I mean. To give up everything again."

We passed an automated tableau of the Last Supper, a crowd of alien-eyed apostles with wind-torn beards moving mechanically, our Savior sitting among them and spreading His arms in benediction. He moved slowly, gracefully, as if swimming through the fog.

"But you're not doing it for Holland, or for me."

He took off his hat, rotating it in his hands like a driver making a long slow turn. "I wouldn't have come to you for that, I wouldn't have ever dared. I tried to let it go and forget, that's what they tell you to do, isn't it? Travel and forget, meet new people and forget. Do you think I sat there all those years and thought: I want to ruin a marriage? If he was happy, if I thought you were happy—"

"Before you came, I thought that I was happy."

He stopped on the boardwalk and looked at me. "That's not the same," he said, "as *being* happy, Pearlie."

We did not move, and so the crowd had to flow around us, some complaining rudely. A peanut vendor bullied his way through the mass of people.

"You called me," Buzz was saying. "You know what you're doing. And it's not for any of us, probably not even for yourself. That's not what you're like."

As the vendor passed us, I saw, reflected in the dented metal of his cart, the two of us standing there together on the boardwalk. I was surprised at how we looked together.

He said: "It's for Sonny. And that I do understand."

"You don't have children," I said, turning away from the image to face the real Buzz.

Buzz grimaced. "No, I don't."

"Then I'm not sure you ever could understand."

"It's why I came to you," he told me, squinting his eyes against the sudden appearance of the sun. "I felt I could trust you. I've been watching you."

When he came to our doorstep with two birthday presents, pretending he was lost, he had been watching me carefully for weeks. Sitting on a bench, or at a bus stop, his collar pulled up, observing little Pearlie Cook, that minor character, as she went about her day. Apparently this is what love will do.

He'd seen me in the mudroom beside the laundry basket—high and wheeled like a perambulator, all steel and Sanforized cotton—dropping clothespins into the sewn-in pocket: a wifely poltergeist, invisibly doing the laundry, the dusting, the dishes. He'd seen me sitting in my own hallway on the chartreuse gossip bench, telephone-talking, and he must have known from the way I played with the nailheads of the upholstery, and pulled at a rip in the leathery vinyl, and cast my eyes up at the ceiling as if the stars were there, that it was Holland I talked to, and what Buzz supposed he recognized, in this static slide show of my life, was someone who would listen.

"And what did you see?" I asked.

"Someone trapped under a heavy stone," he told me. "Someone who would help me."

My story proved it: a girl breaking the law to save a boy from war. An accomplice to a crime, not like other women. Fleeing to the ocean to scrub the yellow paint from her skin, the condemnation of her people, her parents, her country. A criminal who might be called from her retirement, one last time, and not for any fortune he might offer. That would not move her. He would offer a new life, but also the chance, as in her youth, to save someone. She would save her son.

"Help me," Buzz said again.

I am sure we each loved a different man. Because a lover exists only in fragments, a dozen or so if the romance is new, a thousand if we've married him, and out of those fragments our heart constructs an entire person. What we each create, since whatever is missing is filled in by our imagination, is the person we wish him to be. The less we know him, of course, the more we love him. And that's why we always remember that first rapturous night when he was a stranger, and why this rapture returns only when he is dead.

"You've asked for enough already," I told him.

"I must seem like a monster to you."

"And you asked like it was nothing at all."

"I know what it is I'm asking."

Other women did not do this, did not walk this far along the boardwalk with their enemies. They did not knead the red bird in their glove as they talked. They did not abandon their duties, their marriages, their lives like this.

I said: "Have you tried a threat?"

"Pardon?"

"A threat."

He examined me. "What do you mean?"

I glared at him. "You know what I mean."

For a moment I thought I had him. Then he gave the faint flutter of a smile, of admiration, as he made out what was floating through my head. "Blackmail won't work," he said quietly. "Not with me."

"I read up on things."

"I'm giving up my life anyway. I know you're angry. But the police don't frighten me, not anymore. They won't frighten Holland either," he said, unblinking. "Something else is holding him back."

I could feel blood spiking from my heart to my head, like the rhythmic pain I'd had late in carrying Sonny. To be painless, I had thought whenever the throbbing returned to my side; to be painless again is all I ask. In the days since Buzz's late-night visit, I kept wishing for it to stop, only it was not exactly pain; what washed through my blood, at unexpected times, was fear.

I told him, "The other night you said 'someone.'"

He looked at me with very narrow eyes.

"I'm not really the one in the way, am I?"

I amazed us both, there by the seawall. How remarkable we are, in our ability to hide things from ourselves—our conscious minds only a small portion of our actual minds: jellyfish floating on a vast dark sea of knowing and deciding—for even I was startled by what I said next:

"The girl."

If by some miracle I live into a golden era, when racial strife is ended, and time machines are commonplace, and human hearts as clearly charted as the moon, I will travel back and find that young wife by the seawall. I will take her in my old arms and tell her it will be all right. I will tell her that I know she thought she'd learned the awful thing—an old lover come back to claim her husband—yet now here was more, a girl, and everything had come unraveled again. But young wives do not listen to old women. Their fears are so fresh to them; it is inconceivable that everyone has felt them.

"They can't really be carrying on," I said to him.

He paused, thinking how to put it to me. "I need your help, it's complicated."

"How can you still . . . if there's a girl—"

"It doesn't change anything," he said, shaking his head.

I looked at him in absolute astonishment; how could it not change anything? Once again my husband was called into doubt. A girl. Of course it changed everything. A man could not be all things; none of us could be. We did not fit the shape of each container, shifting like water; we were always, unalterably ourselves. Weren't we? And yet there it was, in my mind: the ring of a bicycle bell.

It had always vexed me, hearing that sound each Saturday when Holland gave Annabel DeLawn a ride. It was simple enough: he worked for her father, and was such a favored man that he was given the honor of chauffeuring her to classes at State. I had wondered why she couldn't drive herself; perhaps her father would not allow it, or preferred the notion of a Negro driver. For his princess. So every Saturday when Holland had extra work, and that bell shattered the peace of my day, my husband looked up at me with startled eyes—and then his napkin went down in a crumpled pyramid before he kissed me goodbye. A heart full of worry. Not only because of how it looked, how it had always looked for colored men seen with white women. But because of his beauty. Like the unseen electric force that turns a motor, yet is itself unmoved, his beauty seemed to power this passion in others. It was his naïve talent. But the father was right in his trust; Holland would never knowingly betray it, but the girl herself might. He was innocent, just as the mindless flower is innocent every morning when it opens. That bicycle bell in the front yard; his napkin abandoned on the table; I knew what might happen, with anyone.

"She's an obstacle," he said. "He's at a point in his life where he doesn't know quite who he is or what he wants. He's struggling. He's casting around for options, and she's one of them. You and Sonny are one. And now I've appeared."

"What are you talking about?"

"You wouldn't know it, but he's in a panic. He doesn't know which way he wants his life to go."

"He's not going to *leave* with her—"

"No, but it's a delicate situation."

"Oh, I know all about that. A white girl's not to be trifled with. They make up things." Terrible things, panicked lies. Then I raised my hands in bafflement again. I muttered: "The aunts were right."

"What's that?"

Holland was ill, and never in the ways I had imagined. Bad blood, a crooked heart. It was the sickness of a man floating at sea, half dead in the green light of the oil fires, shouting to the blank horizon just to hear his echo. So he would know he was alive. A man in the hospital, a girl in the neighborhood—it was the same struggle. A ghost breaking dishes so someone will know he's there. I had not saved him; I had only masked the pain like morphine.

We passed by the noisy bumper-car ring. Amid the cries and helium-voiced laughter, I felt its presence: that unnerving sensation of static electricity passing through me on its way to someplace better.

"I don't want to ask you this, but I have to," I said. "Does he have a weak heart?"

"What's that?"

I explained and he looked at me with no judgment at all. It was as if he understood the various flights of fancy someone might have about Holland Cook, the excuses one might invent. But the hospital had pronounced my husband as physically healthy as anyone. There wasn't anything wrong with his heart.

I bit my lip so I would not cry in front of this man. I looked out at a pair of gulls that stood on a column, fighting over a bit of food, gnashing at each other with their red-pipped beaks and losing, with every parry, their tenuous footing.

"Talk to Annabel for me," Buzz whispered in the growing darkness.

"I can't do that."

"Try for me. Woman to woman."

"There's nothing to say. I can't talk to a white girl and ask her to—"

"Just try."

I considered this carefully. I asked a simple thing in return.

We had reached the edge of Playland, where the second roller coaster rose in black reptilian coils above what they called in those days a "dark ride." Over the entrance, in fiery letters, blazed the word LIMBO—and in they went, the laughing teenage couples in their jolting carriages, and out they came, startled and red-faced, lipstick smeared. It was not really a ride for children, not really a haunted house. It was a machine, perhaps like one Buzz and I were constructing, one we have all tried to make, with stories and surprises and romantically lit rooms, a machine meant to force the heart to action. In my mother's day they called it a "tunnel of love."

I watched one white couple emerge from the ride. The girl, in bright makeup and tomboy jeans, her hair mussed wildly around her face, laughed uproariously at something that had just happened, or been said or seen inside. The boy was trying to quiet her, but she kept batting away his hand, shaking her head and laughing. So young, I thought. But it was not true. They were hardly younger than me or Buzz.

I asked him for money. "For Sonny and me."

Buzz said he understood. "But I don't have much cash sitting around. It's invested."

"Considering what you're asking me to—"

"I know, I know. But I have to be careful. That money's all I have. You could take off," he told me. "With Sonny. You could just take off and leave me. And I need you."

"You don't understand," I told him. "How can we just take off?"

He looked at me, blinking, for a moment. "How much do you want?"

I considered this. "A hundred dollars?"

From the look on his face I knew I'd asked for too little. It was a shocked expression, almost amused; he stood digesting what I had said, and then quickly drew out his wallet and began counting money, crisp and green in my hand. I should have asked for more. Two hundred, five hundred, who knows what he could have given me? Who knows what would have been enough? We will never guess our price correctly.

"Look at this," I said, showing him one bill, worn with handling and covered in writing.

"Oh," he said softly in the darkness. "A soldier's dollar."

It was a bill signed by all the members of a division—the Seventh Infantry—as part of a tradition where, before shipping out to Alaska and then to Pearl Harbor, the soldiers all signed a set of dollar bills and headed to a bar to spend them. You used to come across these dollars all the time in San Francisco, though they were rare by 1953. A way for those doomed boys to be remembered, a scrap of immortality.

"It's getting dark," I said.

"Trust me, Pearlie," he said as he turned to buy me a soda. There was no need to say that. All alone out in the Sunset, I had to trust a rich white man. There was no one else to turn to.

Buzz spoke with the vendor, his profile stark against the ocean, the break in his nose more apparent than ever. Our bargain: that this would be the face Holland would see first thing in the morning and last thing at night, wherever they decided to live. They say there are many worlds, populated by the different paths we take in life, and in any other one, Buzz would have been the enemy. But I had seen the dangers, and picked my side. There was no other world for me but this one. Treaties shift according to the war, and to release Sonny from this madhouse, I was willing to accept, if not friendship with this man, at least a cautious truce.

I looked around at that old faded amusement park. It is gone now. Taken down years ago, after the place had gone sour and dark around the edges, the broken parts of the rides never replaced, the caramel corn reheated and reused until nobody bought it anymore. It was old-fashioned by then, part of a lost time: funhouse mirrors that warped the normal world; sudden drafts that blew girls' skirts into the air; the thrilling jolts and shocks of the rides themselves—they tore free, somehow, into a country where everything became warped, and shocking, and upside down. The fun and freedom; the terror and restraint; only the ocean was left behind. Torn down—and burned down, parts of it, by owners desperate enough to make a final penny from junky old Playland-by-the-Sea. I am not saying that I loved it or miss it; you could never have caged a frenzy like that forever. I am only saying that it's gone.

"This is lunacy," I said to Buzz. "I think I should just talk to Holland."

"No," he said, very firmly.

I asked, "Why not?"

"I'll . . . I'll handle Holland."

"I'm his wife," I said haughtily, drawing myself up beside the seawall. "I think I know him well enough."

We both stood in silence at the utter ridiculousness of this statement. All around us, families came and went with balloons and stuffed toys in their hands, faces marred with chocolate and ice cream. I began to laugh at the absurdity of it all and could not stop. It was the shock and relief of a storm cloud bursting open with rain. I leaned against the vendor's cart and gasped for breath, laughing helplessly until I saw that Buzz was laughing, too. He shook his head and sniffed in amusement. And that was the first time that I felt it. As we found our breath and stared at each other, sighing: the peculiar bond between us.

Sunset had arrived, barely pinking up the fog. And at last, the lights came on across the length of Playland, a thousand bulbs or more, flashing along the roller coaster curves, and lighting up the shoreline of our city in a way that would have made us a welcoming target during the war. The instinct to turn them off was still strong, left over from a vanished world. Because this was a time of blessed peace.

And then Buzz did a very surprising thing. He turned to me, motleyed by the flash of fairground lights, and took my hand in his. I struggled, seeing myself as others passing on the boardwalk saw me: a colored woman, poorly dressed, eagerly talking with a handsome white man. No one would have known, from how he held my hand, that this man planned to take my husband from me. That over the years of heartache he had hatched a plot to change my life forever. He held his grip and would not let me go. I do not know what joins the parts of an atom, but it seems what binds one human to another is pain.

I did not know what to think of Ethel Rosenberg, the Jewish wife convicted of helping her husband hand nuclear secrets to the Soviets. In speckled trial photographs, her face seemed hard as a porcelain doll's, her body stiff with anger, dressed in the outdated hat and cloth coat of a poor woman. It was difficult to think of her as a mother. She was forced to wear the shame of the whole affair—even her own brother stood witness against her at her trial—and when finally she was sentenced to death, no relative would accept her children. They were to be orphaned. The general consensus at the time was that Ethel had let this happen, the ungrateful Jewish woman, deceiving the very nation that had liberated her race, had let her children be orphaned, her family name ruined, all because she would not speak against her madman husband. Even my neighbor Edith could not bear the disgrace.

The cabinets have been unlocked now, the government papers, yellow with age, have been released; her now-dead brother's confession has been heard and we know the truth: that Ethel Rosenberg, born Ethel Greenglass, was no spy. But it changes nothing, for no one claimed she was a spy. She was sentenced to death, as the judge put it, because she did not "deter" her husband. Her handsome Julius, sworn to revolution. The judge said that her silence—not her actions, but her silence—had altered the course of history, that a weak-chinned Jewish wife with a lovely singing voice had brought about the Korean War, the rise of communism, the death of so many of our soldiers, and perhaps the end of the world. Delinquent wives will hasten our ruin. And so she had to die.

"Hold me close," Ethel wrote to her husband in Sing Sing, "my heart is heavy with wanting you." What charmed circle had he drawn around her to keep her silence? As I read their passionate letters, and imagined her singing "Goodnight, Irene" to him from her adjacent cell, and stared at their photographed kiss, I longed to feel something for her. The good wife. The bad American. The bad mother. She looked, in her mug shot, like a woman from the last century: shirtwaist and cameo, hair wild and unset, an immigrant just arrived from a burning country, her eyes looking past the camera as if her vision pierced through walls and saw the chair awaiting her. Lips pursed in some twisted fervor that was worth her very life, her sons' lives, worth all our lives. Silent, still silent long after it could be of any help to anybody. Who was she fighting for? Her beloved Julius? Herself?

"Poor Ethel," was all I could manage to whisper, and my husband would look up from his clipped newspaper and put his hand on my arm: "Colored folks got their own problems." That was true enough.

Holland Cook kissed me goodbye every morning at eight and hello every evening at six, as lovely and regular as the phases of the moon. I iced his drinks from the same howling freezer, pinned up his same laundry, and ironed our world as stiff and flat as ever. He held my hand and smiled at me with the sweetness of an old lover, and I smiled back. And yet none of it was real; after Buzz's declaration, our movements felt like those of mechanical people once a penny is dropped in the slot. Or better: figures from a dream.

Today any woman would leave him, but divorce in those days meant finding legal grounds. Insanity, intemperance. There was always, of course, adultery, but the aunts' stories had taught me how difficult getting the proof could be. In my doubt about Annabel, I considered following the lovers out to some trysting place, my husband and his supposed mistress fogging up the Plymouth with their eager breath. But Buzz persuaded me it was a crazed idea. There is no good explanation for why love compels this of us: that we must seek out and witness the very scenes that would destroy us.

Despite these mad revelations, I could not leave him. He was not just Buzz's first love, he was mine as well, and so we shared that famous sickness; it ebbed and flowed through our blood like malaria. Who could leave until the last moment, and even beyond that, when he might still turn around and reach for her? Who wouldn't wait for change long after change is possible?

I tried to convince myself I was past caring. Each cup of coffee, each starched shirt and matched sock; the thousand cords that bound me to my husband. I pictured a hot-air balloon bound to the earth. One by one, I thought, with these simple automatic tasks, I would undo each cord. This shame and panic in my heart would pass; I would feel it growing, daily, more buoyant. Free from pain. In a month, three months, I might scarcely care what happened to him at all.

And so our routine continued. It was early one evening; he and Sonny played on the living-room rug, toys spread out before them. The favorite was a paratrooper that, when tossed in the air, unfurled to reveal a parachute, printed with a hawk, as it floated gently to the carpet. Lyle, unfortunately, had gotten to the parachute and torn it to loving pieces, so Holland had to repair it with an old bread bag and some string. I had given Sonny my metal belt to play with. From the radio came talk of the war: the president, promising an end was near, that even those still being drafted were unlikely to see action.

I looked at my husband's silhouette against the window; it had not changed. A memory; another knot to untie quietly: "Holland, you remember your room back in Childress?"

He turned to face me, saying nothing. His hair spiral-gleamed with pomade. The radio began to talk about a movie star.

"I don't know what made me think of that," I said, my face warm as he stared at me. "You remember how there was that one rip in the shade and we'd tell the time that way?"

"I don't know I do . . ."

I touched his arm and smiled. "You took your mumblety-peg knife and you stabbed it in the desk and drew a little sundial around it and we'd watch it to know when the piano lesson was supposed to be up. And I'd stop reading to you. And your mother would come upstairs. You don't remember that?"

Sonny started talking to his soldiers.

Holland looked down at my hand and covered it with his. "I remember you reading to me."

"Mommy," Sonny said. "It broke."

"I'll fix it," I said, taking the belt and slipping it into the pocket of my dress.

"Poetry," he said. "Countee Cullen."

I asked which one.

"About the box of gold." Then my husband did an amazing thing. It was akin to having the moon, which has lit every night of your young life, revolve in the sky and smile down at you. He stared at the floor in deep concentration and murmured: "I have wrapped my dreams . . ." I was a girl again.

His bronze face beamed with the pride of having memorized those poems in his long days of hiding. He began another: "I have a rendezvous with life—" then closed his eyes with sudden pain, leaning away from me into his armchair. He handed the soldier he had mended to Sonny, who threw him high into the air. The name "Yreka Bakery" floated above us for a breathless moment. Sonny was overjoyed, and wanted to try it again, but Holland said, "I don't feel so well."

"Is it your heart?" I asked very sharply.

All those years I asked about your heart, did you guess the harmless lie I had invented for myself? Or did you simply accept it as a quirk of mine? As full of wonder at my mysteries as I was of yours, forgiving them as willingly: two veiled people, leading each other hand in hand. Perhaps this is a marriage. You said, "I'm going to lie down for a minute. You think Lyle wants to join me?"

"I'm sure."

"Lyle, you crazy thing, you want a lie-down?"

You deserved your rest. Men like you, who had risked their lives and seen the worst of human life, never wanted to talk about fear or think about it; you had fought for the freedom never to mention such things, not even to your private self. The shame I had felt; it must have pierced you deeper, letting the ocean water in. I had tried to understand it, and mistook for a transposed heart something either very simple—the secret of your life with that white man—or something far harder to comprehend. A search for some relief; a respite from the life you had.

A little lie-down. No more than any of us wanted—after the Depression, and the war. After all we had been through together, sacrificed for each other. This offer Buzz had made me. This man now falling asleep on our marital couch. Perhaps this was the all clear we had been waiting for.

But tell me—what scene played before your eyes when you lay with your mute dog, arranging himself at your feet? What comforted you on your way to sleep? Was it the shade drawn over your boyhood window with the glow of a shut eyelid? Or a hospital window, its shade pulled up to light a man in love?

Sonny was the kind of boy who held my hand as we walked, every day, to the playground, where babies cloudgazed from black old-fashioned prams and older children beat at the cold hard sand of the sandbox until it was soft as silk. Sonny never took part in any of this. He approached the park as cautiously as if it were a lake. A few steps and he was in up to his knees, then his waist, stopping to get used to the sensation (half in a dream, imagining waves softly soaking his clothes), then he would smile and produce a toy from his pocket—a soldier, a pig—and set it on the grass before him. All the time, his eye was on the other children. He never came close to their orbit. He would not be drawn in. He sensed, as the only child who wasn't white, an unvoiced law, and (still an obedient boy) he would abide by it.

The hundred dollars Buzz gave me was quickly spent. I treated Sonny to trips to the zoo, the park, to an adventure on the L line: the tram, with its buttery shell and carved-out windows, seemed to him a rolling jack-o'-lantern. It took us a few blocks down Taravel to an upscale candy shop that I had spotted, near the Parkside movie theater. At the front, where a carved-wood Indian might have guarded a cigar store, stood an iron-and-glass gumball machine. A little boy took a penny from his fat, friendly mother and dropped it in, clearly hoping for a "ringer" that would set off a bell and win him a full-size candy bar. "Dang it," he murmured as another ordinary ball clinked down, bumblebee-striped. The mother's arms were crossed; they had been at this for some time.

The elderly shop owner was a relic: ruddy and mustachioed, chewing his dentures, pants suspendered above a round belly. He asked if he could help us and I smiled and said we were getting something for my son; the man frowned at me over his glasses. I leaned down to Sonny and asked, "Which do you want?" I caught the mother's prying eye as Sonny took in the store and its expanse of wonders.

Luminous jars along the counter offered a seemingly endless supply of delight: long ropes of Bub's Daddy gum in nuclear-age reds, greens, and purples; wax lips, fangs, and mustaches that could be worn only for a hilarious minute or two before puncturing and leaking an odious liquor into your mouth; flying saucers made of crisp tasteless wafers; Saf-T-Pops with the handle made into a ring (so kids might trip, but not choke) nestled among the real McCoys of bright handmade lollipops suffocating in their loose cellophane hoods; bubble-gum cigars and pistols for young hoodlums; lipstick candies that no boy would dare purchase; and, looped in their clean glass jar like nooses, my father's favorite and his grandson's horror, coils of blackjack licorice.

Sonny studied the jars carefully, like a Chinese physician examining his potions. He stared for a long time at the sugared fruits before choosing some cherries, the bland saucers, a pyramid of caramels, and others. They were delicately pulled from their jars (rare fish from a tank) until at last they lay glowing on the wax paper before him. Sonny, hands clasped, regarded them with awe.

The owner did not move at all but just said, "Those are fancy ones, you realize."

"I can pay."

"I hope you can."

A long stare that neither of us broke. I slammed a five-dollar bill onto the counter, making the candy canes shake.

My son paused then whispered: "Which one can I keep?"

I wish I had a photograph of his face. The stunned look, within which one could easily see, like the developing details on a photographic plate, the image of his father. Which one? All of them, I meant to tell him, all of them from now until forever. There will be enough of everything. But my child had not yet comprehended his mistake, nor had the horrible man, so I looked up at that white mother, stuffed into her blue cloth coat, and caught her staring, entranced, at my cautious son, while her ungrateful lout dropped one accursed penny after another into his slot machine.

I brought myself down to the level of my son's eyes, so serious, full of his prudent question, and I waited, savoring the moment, imagining those eyes brightening at what I was about to say.

If you went to a soda fountain today and said "I'll have a Suicide," the owner would probably call the police. But in an earlier day the soda jerk, his Adam's apple working hard with every swallow, would have pistol-pointed his finger and said, "Sure thing, pardner." A fluted glass under the fountain, the release of carbonated Coca-Cola, and then, going down the row, a trickle of poison from every flavor—chocolate, cherry, vanilla—until you had an ink-black beverage set before you, ruffled with foam and smelling like a potion. For this, a nickel.

That is what William the Seltzer Boy made for Annabel DeLawn at Hussey's Colonial Creamery, a black flap of hair falling over his left eye, big hands resting on the pulls as he watched her drop a dime on the counter and make her way to a booth where her friend was waiting. Carbonation sparkled in the soda-shop air. Tacked to the wall, an auto-supply calendar left open to a month in 1943; possibly the man who used to tear the pages had gone to war and not come back, the modern version of those pocket watches in murder mysteries that always crack and fail at the hour of death.

I sat two pews behind Annabel, quiet as a widow in church, in the back of the shop where Mr. Hussey preferred his Negroes. A weary soldier smiled across from me, nursing his root beer as if it were real beer. What was I drinking? A lemon phosphate, thank you, William—tablet in a glass, quickly drowned by a flood of fizzing water. A decent married woman's order. I forced myself to ignore William, the ugly term he muttered as I left. And there I sat, hidden in the shadow of a column, in my best hat and coat with the phosphate pricking my nose and glowing like an anti-dote. I had planned my confrontation only to realize we are as cowardly with rivals as with those loved from afar.

She was not beautiful. I decided that immediately as I saw her puckering her lips over the stiff red tip of the straw. But she had managed, with her sharp nose, her filbert-shaped face visibly freckled beneath the powder (flecks of vanilla in the cream), to create an illusion of beauty. A plain white girl who had learned to act as if she were pretty. The way she sat: mermaid-like, with her legs drawn up beneath her, and her voice modulated with a deli-cate ring that rose, now and then, into laughter the way my grand-mother's porch chime often broke into a wind-busied clangor. Her charm bracelet also rang, mostly with light, as its various hearts, books, and anchors caught the sun, and a single silver ring hung gleaming on her breast like an acrobat's hoop. All the time, as she chatted with her friend, she drummed on her ziggurat of school-books with a brush-tipped eraser.

"White with navy polka dots, and the top is navy with white polka dots."

"Sounds lovely, doll."

"I hope so, it cost a pretty penny."

She was not what I'd thought she would be, nor what I'd hoped. I had imagined a cute, simpering airhead, not a bright girl

desperate for something greater than life in our Sunset. Over-
hearing her conversation, I learned Annabel was studying chemistry at State in an astounding fantasy that a woman could be a
scientist in 1953. That is what she talked about, as her friend tried
to tempt her with sillier topics, as her straw went in and out of her
Suicide: those chemistry classes, and the professors who ridiculed
her, her disapproving father and the male students who pinched
her. She talked about it all with humor, but the strain was already
showing in the tired circles that her makeup could not hide.

"You won't guess what they put in my lab notebook."

"Oh, I don't want to know."

"Dirty pictures of course. Filthy, filthy pictures."

"Annabel, what did you do?"

"Said it was hilarious, of course. What else could I do? You
can't let them know they've got you."

A burst of birdlike laughter: a young married white couple
across from Annabel, the bride very pregnant, the groom very
dusty. They were clearly passing through; I could see their road-
mangled car sleeping by the curb, bags tied to the top. Inside, a
dog readjusted its position of longing. They had come far to escape the Nebraska of their license plate, and who knows what
surefire plan they'd cooked up in Mexico or Alaska? Seeing them,
I could not help but feel an American stab of hope.

From the booth, a familiar name.

The friend produced a waterfall of mirth: "Isn't that rich?"

"Where did you hear that?" Annabel asked, looking around
but not catching sight of me. "There's nothing to it, I'm sure."

"I thought you'd know all about it!" and more silvery laughter
followed. "A married woman carrying on beneath her husband's
nose—"

"Hush, I've never even met his wife." Annabel DeLawn turned
to her dark cupcake and, picking at its pleated silver skirt with her
nails, began to undress it on the table like a doll. William ran past
me to get something from a back room.

Then her friend added, in a whisper: "A *Negro*, of all things."
"I said hush."

"And that husband of hers so gorgeous like a movie star." Giggling: "Well you'd know all about that, wouldn't you, Annabel?"

"Let's change the topic."

The silver foil of Annabel's cake caught the light in a kind of fireworks, tossing blue sequins around the room. I thought I heard her sigh.

I felt the broken belt in my pocket and a brief, embarrassing fantasy occurred to me: at Playland again, following my husband and Annabel out to the Limbo ride—that tunnel of love—where they would board the hearse-shaped cars and enter, hands clasped, its great gaping mouth. Wildly, absurdly, I imagined I sat in the car behind them, listening to their whispers and echoed laughter. A scream—a giant spider above them. And then, all at once, the power would go out. Darkness, silence. Bird in the hand. I imagined a perfect crime: that of climbing from my car, pulling the belt from my pocket and slipping it around her neck. It felt, in the innocence of my daydream, like a passionate embrace; it was the struggle I had never had: that of never-letting-go, not for something that you want so much, not until the thing is done. Never-letting-go.

We should forgive ourselves the cruelty of our youth. I wasn't that much older than Annabel, though I thought of myself as a grown-up married woman. I was young and in anguish, and she was young and struggling to make the best of her lot as a woman, and of the times she lived in. Glittering with charm and keeping that bitter smile as wide as she could. Surely she was as afraid as I was. And who knows what those rides with my husband meant, in truth—a husband casting about for options, finding it perhaps in this poor girl—and what Buzz's jealousy, like an imp taking the form of our worst fears, had summoned.

From the booth: "Oh, Annabel, you tease. Tell me about him."

"I won't! I'm sure you know I'm promised to someone else!"

"But you're not married yet."

"Why should we? We're keeping it secret, and I want to finish my studies first."

"You're a riot, Annabel, a regular riot!"

In irritation: "Gotta go, hon."

Across from her, the bride gave out a gasp; from a tipped-over canister flowed the pink lava of a shake. William Platt ran from the back and grabbed a rag at the fountain.

Annabel passed a hand through her hair and the little charms on her bracelet tinkled like bells; the promise ring on her breastbone caught the light. Then, for a moment, I thought she saw me. Her body went straight and clean as a lighthouse, her eyes moving across the room, and her gaze seemed headed right for me. I felt that I might do it; I might talk to her. But her eyes moved over me and around the room until they settled on William, running by with his rag. He grinned and she smiled back, brightly, like a switch he had flicked on with his finger. Then with a bell she was through the door and gone, just a ghost haunting the window as she stopped outside to ask a policeman a question, her finger tracing the glowing French curve of her hair.

" 'Scuse me folks."

It was William, arriving with his bar rag, quickly wiping up the tabletop with the same circular caress I had seen him use to wash the family Ford, dotingly, soapily, on semi-sunny days. The pregnant girl held both hands up in a gesture of compliance, smiling, not as her husband smiled (with embarrassment) but with the pleasure some pregnant women have at being a bit of trouble to the world, and she watched the soda jerk as he cleaned. Around and around he went. And all the time his happy gaze was on the window, on Annabel. After a minute, she flashed her teeth at the helpful policeman and fled, her progress down the street reflected now only as a smirking glint in the cop's girl-watching eye and a glowing one in William's.

When he was done, handsome William (the basketball star) threw the rag into a distant bucket, wiped his hands on his apron,

and, turning around and seeing my foam-ringed glass, picked up
the empty thing—one finger of his right hand whitened by an ab-
sent ring—and looked right at me with the doomed sweet smile
of a boy in love.

Buzz invited me to his office for our next meeting. We toured vast
aviaries of chirping apparatuses, where workers lowered heavy
patterns onto bolts of cloth and others fed huge blind cutting machines their daily feast of fabric. Buzz explained that during the
war his father had altered the corset factory to sew parachutes for
flares. "War is never what you think it will be," he said, leading me
across a high catwalk made of metal strips—like walking on the
teeth of a comb—and when at last we had completed our circuit,
he turned to me with his hands on his hips and grinned broadly.
"That's it!" he shouted. "What do you think?"

The machines entered a new round of gonging and Buzz
shouted something else I could not hear. I shook my head and he
repeated it.

"I'm selling it, I'm selling everything!" he shouted, grinning,
then took a breath as if puzzled, perhaps hurt I had not divined
his purpose. He had shown me his empire. The whirring menag-
erie his family had brought to life. He looked at me for a long moment, his lips slightly open, with the machines buzzing and clanging
all around, waiting for me to understand.

"For you!" he exclaimed at last over the noise, his hands flying
out before him.

We stood, facing each other, as the battle noise rose around us.
Like allies in a fairy tale, each with half of a broken locket, now
Buzz and I had shown each other the depths of our sacrifice, the
treasures we were willing to surrender so they might fit together.
Mine was a story of my youth, the home I had lost for my hus-
band. And here was his: bright and oiled and twittering around

me. Not just the brick aerodrome and the machines it enclosed, the precision instruments for making precision garments, but the family history he was willing to part with forever—no less than what I, myself, had relinquished. Buzz said it was for me, but that was not exactly true. It was for Holland.

A hundred thousand dollars, more or less. That was what the factory and the various businesses were worth. It was also the exact sum, in *Double Indemnity*, that Fred MacMurray told Barbara Stanwyck she could get if they killed her husband, did him in "straight down the line." In 1953, it might as well have been a million.

We passed through a heavy door and, with a creak and a slam of relief, the din was silenced, replaced by the cricketing of well-oiled Singers attended by women in kerchiefs and overalls. One woman's station was set with gleaming metal slivers, like the table of a knife thrower; apparently she was adding boning to the corsets. I said: "Reminds me of the first job I had in the war."

"And what was that?"

"Wrapping fighter jets in paper."

He laughed aloud. "That's not a real job! That's a job from the funnies."

"That was really my job," I said, feeling slightly defensive. "That's why they brought us from Kentucky, the colored women, to wrap jets in paper. They needed the labor and we needed . . . don't laugh."

"I'm sorry."

"They shipped them out to the Pacific, you'd think they'd fly them out, but they didn't, and they wanted them all shiny and new for the boys. Four of us would climb up ladders with huge sheets of brown paper and we'd tape them together. Some girls would leave notes inside for the men to read, phone numbers." Now it was my turn to laugh. "It was absurd. But it was better than welding steel, better on your eyes. I remember the welding girls all had to drink milk to purge the poisons from their systems."

"But why wrap planes?" he asked again, baffled. "They were headed to war. Who cares how shiny the planes are?"

I said that war is never what you expect it to be.

Buzz laughed at that, then looked down on his workers in their droning underworld. The woman picked up her little knives, one by one, and slipped them in the pockets of a corset. That was when I told him I hadn't confronted Annabel. Buzz grimaced in the half-light, and when he did that, I knew he had not come to me, that dark night, so I would "remove" Annabel for him. He hoped it would work, but he knew me; he'd watched me; he must have guessed I had no magic touch with girls like her, sipping Suicides in segregated shops. There was something more. What did he really want? Perhaps love is a minor madness. And as with madness, it is unendurable alone. The one person who can relieve us is of course the sole person we cannot go to: the one we love. So instead we seek out allies, even among strangers and wives, fellow patients who, if they can't touch the edge of our particular sorrow, have felt something that cuts nearly as deep.

"We'll find another way," he said softly.

"I'm sorry. They were foolish gossips, those girls. Annabel and her friend."

"It's all right."

I recited a line about those kind of girls, and it took Buzz a moment to realize I was quoting Holland's favorite poet.

"You're full of surprises, Pearlie Cook," he told me.

"I hope I am."

"Not too many, please."

"She thinks we're lovers, by the way," I said suddenly. "You and me, it's crazy. There's some rumor going around the neighborhood—"

"I wouldn't worry about that."

"Well I don't like being talked about."

"They always talk about the wrong things, anyway. They never know what's really going on."

"I did overhear she's promised to a young man."

"Promised?"

"It's what young people are doing. Before engagement, you're promised."

He seemed baffled, amused. "But engagement is the promise."

"I can't say I understand it. A vow, endlessly diluted."

"Maybe it allows them to neck. People have some funny codes," he shrugged. "Who's the promised man?"

There was a clatter downstairs as a woman dropped her thread clippers and the floorwalker ran over to get her back in line. Buzz watched the women very carefully, then calmly asked me again.

I said the name. Bottles being set down on our front step every morning. That clear glass sound. A ring gleaming on her breast-bone, and the wide smile on his face as she departed.

"William Platt, the Seltzer Boy," he said. "How wholesome." And I laughed. He took my arm and led me into a great loud room where they boxed up everything, and from there into a small, beautifully furnished parlor with a long mirror at one end and a folding screen at the other. Some soundproofing substance erased the screaming machines; you would never have known there was a factory outside that door. It felt like the house of a maiden aunt. From the center of the ceiling hung an incongruous lamp in the shape of a bird in flight. Buzz crossed the room and pressed a white porcelain button set into the wall.

"William Platt . . ." Buzz repeated. On the wall behind him hung the framed image of a Gibson Girl, her enhanced bustline (WE FIX FLATS!) attracting the attention of a cartoonish dough-boy; characters from our parents' bygone age. Then his forehead creased. "Why is he still here?"

"Well he's got two jobs, seltzer delivery on Saturdays and—"

"No, I mean still around at all." He smiled sadly and gestured to the doorway, beyond which older men sat cutting at their forms. "I don't see a lot of young men around these days, do you?" He was right; the last figure I had heard was thirty thousand boys a month were going to fight in Korea. And this despite our president saying the war was over. "He's not a college boy, is he just lucky?" He pressed the button again. "Miss Johnson isn't answering. I wanted to find you a gift." I said I didn't need anything, I should be going.

"Tell me, Pearlie," he said suddenly, those blue eyes flashing. "Tell me what you think I should do."

What gave him the right to ask such a question? He did not want help with Annabel, not exactly; nor did he merely want me to move aside. What he wanted me to be, of all amazing things, was my husband's procuress.

"You can't ask me that," I said.

He frowned and shook his head. "But you know him better than anyone," he said, looking kindly up at me.

I was a girl again, before a powerful man. I stood in my father's farmhouse back in Kentucky, in my plain dress, tormented by the past but flattered, listening to Mr. Pinker describe the wonders of California, the enormous planes that women like me were to wrap in paper, how America needed me, how I could do a favor for him. Such a small favor. The gold lapel pin gleaming in the humid light. To tell everybody's secrets, even invented ones.

How do you make someone love you? For the very young, there can be nothing harder in the world. You may try as hard as you like: place yourself beside them, cook their favorite food, bring them wine or sing the love songs that you know will move them. They will not move them. Nothing will move them. You will waste days interpreting the simple banalities of a phone call; months staring at their soft lips as they talk; you will waste years watching a body sitting in a chair and willing every muscle to take you across the room and do a simple thing, say a simple word, make them love you, and you will not do it; you will waste long nights wondering how they cannot feel this—the urge to embrace, the snowmelt in the heart when you are near them—how they can sit in that chair, or speak with those lips, or make a call and mean nothing by it, hide nothing in their hearts. Or perhaps what they hide is not what you want to see. Because surely they love someone. It simply isn't you.

But when you are older, there are ways. The young think better possibilities are everywhere, better lovers, better lives; by twenty-five or thirty, options have dwindled; life has shrunk. All you have to do is limit those options to one, just whittle life to a point.

And what is left at that point? You are, Buzz Drumer. You are left.

I can't explain the strangeness of thinking of my husband in this way. I felt like a magician who has decided to retire, and one afternoon, over a drink, tells a younger man all of the secrets to his lifetime of tricks. It has a false bottom, a secret pane of glass; the smoke obscures the wires. Only the difference was that I had never thought of these as tricks; I had merely thought of it as a marriage, the secret panes and wires we use to keep up the pleasantest illusion on earth, and the ways in which I had won and kept him, though carefully done, had come to seem as artless as any romance. Perhaps they were. But like the magician, I balked at saying these things. Not because they were such great secrets but because, in telling them, I knew my role as a wife would be over. Yet I thought of that heart—beating on the wrong side of my husband's chest—and I thought of my son.

I asked if Buzz had kept anything from their time together, perhaps as a gift, something to summon the past. He looked at me sadly.

"Of course I did," he said. He must have had a drawerful of such mementos, a curated collection to first love. Of course he did.

There was a sound from the factory; a surge of electricity made the bird glow brightly and I could not explain why my eyes began to well with tears.

To give up a marriage—someone unmarried might imagine it's

like giving up a seat in a theater, or sacrificing a trick in bridge for the possibility of better, later. But it is harsher than anyone could realize: a hot invisible fire, burning pieces of hope and fantasy, and charred bits of the past. It had to go, however, if something were to be built in its place. So I stood there and gave Buzz advice, and all I could think of were the automatons we had seen at Playland, moving beautifully in the wind, and the children who were taken behind the scenes on a tour and shown, to their surprise, the vast tangle of wires and switches that would be so hard to undo, and even worse, once undone, to bring to life again.

When Holland's birthday came at last, we had a little party and invited the aunts, who burst through the door full of excitement. "We've got good and bad news," the eldest announced, shaking rain from her like a poodle. "But what horrible, horrible news!"

Alice turned to me, hand on my shoulder, in the polite semblance of inclusion. For some reason, only she wore an orchid on her breast: "Pearlie, you must have heard about it—"

"You can see from her face! Well it happened in Fresno, I think last night—"

"Oh hello Holland! Happy birthday, honey! And there's baby Walter—"

"Oh kiss your aunt Bea, Walter, I ain't contagious—"

The younger took advantage of her sister's distraction: "A fourteen-year-old white girl murdered her twin sister!"

I smiled; this was the kind of news they had discouraged me from talking about in front of their nephew. Holland was removing their long alpaca coats, beaded with rain, to reveal similar Wrinkl-Shed dresses. Sonny was staring at me as each aunt caressed him in turn.

Beatrice continued, talking as if there had been no break: "Got her brother's gun, in the dark, mind you, felt her way along the bed until she touched her sister's hair and her right ear and she put the shotgun—"

"It was a rifle. It was a twenty-two."

They glowed in the telling of the twins' nightmare, narrating like actual witnesses, heedless of what a small boy might make of their gruesome details: a girl's hand feeling its way along the sheets, inch by inch, touching the soft coils of her more-perfect sister's hair, then her skull, then descending the springy rubber steps of her ear . . . it took me a few moments before I realized they were talking about a radio show.

"Now ladies—" Holland interrupted, winking at me.

"But it was based on a true story, dear! It really did happen in Fresno! And things like this happen all the time in Fresno!"

"Do they?" I asked.

"And do you know what? She did it because she never liked her."

Alice: "Imagine that. Never liking your twin!"

Beatrice: "And to *murder* her!"

A burble of laughter as they degloved their soft hands.

We moved to the living room and the night was so cool and rainy that someone suggested a fire. Sonny was completely taken by how his father built it for him, Boy Scout–style, in the fireplace. The aunts hummed to each other as the fire rose to a crackle, watching as Holland opened each gift. They squeezed their faces in pleasure, identically, together, and looked right into each other's smiling eyes. I wondered who wanted to murder the other the most.

Holland served us drinks, and they started telling us other minor gossip—it amazed me that they moved so smoothly from astonishment to chatter—and also something in the paper about a visiting Dutch psychologist who claimed "nations have souls."

"Dr. Zeylmans van Emmichoven!" one aunt proclaimed in a flash of recall.

The other explained: "You see, psycho-logic-ally we're a real young country. When Europeans visit us here, and Africans of course, they feel real old because their nations are so old. Psychologic-ally. Hundreds, hundreds of years older than us."

"It's because we're young we do things in a big way," said the first. "Like the A-bomb, and the H-bomb that's coming. We have a youthful drive." And, laughing, she added: "Well I certainly feel young!"

"Isn't that interesting," Holland said, but I just listened to them. Those girls mystified me. I had never felt young in that way. I had never felt American, either.

The older sister gave her a glance, then said, "And an inner kindness. He says America has an inner kindness." She began to wad her napkin and nod, not looking at anybody. "It sure makes a lot of sense to me."

"I'm too hot," Sonny said quietly to me.

I told him to turn away from the fire, which he did with a smile of regret.

That was when Buzz appeared, soaked to the bone. Holland introduced him, and the twins paused for a chilling second. At the time, I thought the scene in the doorway meant the destruction of all their careful plans for their nephew, that place out in the Sunset, the advice to his new wife, their constant vigilance at our house. I have to admit: I felt a little sorry to have let them down.

They said of course they knew Buzz. He used to be Holland's boss back before Pearlie. "Am I his boss now?" I asked. They stared at me quite hopelessly.

"It's bad out!" Buzz said, grinning. "Real bad. Happy birthday, everyone. Holland, I've brought you a present."

"I haven't returned your first present to the store yet!"

Laughter. "Now you can return them together," Buzz said.

He produced it from his rain-spangled coat and handed it to Holland: a small box, wrapped in the same bright turquoise as my bird-in-hand gloves.

Holland squinted as he took it.

"It's nothing special. It's just something I found around the old place," Buzz said. "Open it."

Sonny asked what old place? And the aunts, those nervous busybodies, said never you mind.

What did they know? What did they guess?

I found myself watching Holland's face the entire time he undid the ribbon and wrapping and lifted off the lid. It was the expression I had caught that day Buzz arrived, when my husband came down the stairs and found his old lover drinking beer with his wife. It was the look of a man who feels the presence of a ghost.

He sat for a moment with the tissue hanging from the box. I looked at Buzz and saw his eyes widen in expectation. "Well will you look at that," my husband said at last. He pulled out an ugly little wooden object. He laughed. "It's the old pipe bird."

"That's right," Buzz said, closing his eyes and turning away from Holland's awkward smile, just as Sonny had turned from another fire.

My husband paused a moment, an archaeologist examining a treasure long since thought lost, before showing the bird to his son and, with a flick of his thumb, opening its head on a hinge to reveal the compartment where, neatly tucked inside, lay the bowl of a pipe. Another flick and the bowl was hidden, the pipe stem now camouflaged as a tail. Sonny was captivated and wanted to have it, but his father pocketed it and patted his head.

"You can play with it later," he said.

"Can we play moody room?" his son asked.

"Not now."

Sonny turned to me, the appeals court. It was a favorite game where my son stood in each corner of the room and we guessed the emotion he enacted. My little boy in his leg braces that made him march like a soldier around the room, telling Lyle to get out of the way as he prepared himself for each round, his face drawn close in concentration. Leaping before the wallpaper, body clenched, as we yelled "Anger!" or "Madness!" or "Passion!"

"Later on, after dinner," I said, and his father handed him a toy soldier with a parachute. Up it went into the air: Yreka Bakery. I was startled once again by how Buzz had entered my husband's heart. I wondered if my son felt the change. Children are so sensitive, like bees to the health of their queen who lose their purpose when she falls ill, wandering through the combs until the hive collapses. I watched my son focusing so hard on the floating soldier. Could he feel something at the center of our family dying?

It was after the birthday cake that the older aunt stood up and said, "I have a little announcement."

Holland made a joke about his aunts and their announcements.

"No, this one's quite serious," she said. Her sister was acting very oddly, curling up in her seat and pressing the orchid to her nose and glancing all around the room with a faint smile. We'd had nothing but beer at dinner; I wondered if the aunts had taken something stronger before they arrived. "The good news I was telling you about."

"Well what is it, Bea? We're in suspense," Holland said, smiling.

Beatrice cleared her throat and, without looking at her sister, proclaimed there was going to be a wedding.

"What?" Holland said, laughing into his napkin. "You're joking."

"It's no joke," said the elder very sternly. "Alice is getting married."

"Well who's she marrying?"

They named someone I had never heard of, and Holland slapped his hand on the table in disbelief. Sonny, making no sense of all this, tried to go for another piece of cake before I stopped him, and he glared at me in hatred.

The elder aunt proclaimed that her sister was in love and that was that.

Buzz caught my eye, very amused by it all.

"But you can't get married! At your age . . ."

"Holland! You're acting like a child. It's a beautiful occasion and I want you to kiss Alice and congratulate her."

He stood up and kissed his aunt, who was not really his aunt, but all he had left of his family. It must have shaken him to see the presumably petrified aunts capable of change. Even the Rock of Gibraltar might topple. "I'm so happy for you," he told her, and she fairly glittered with pleasure. He smiled and patted her shoulder warmly, and the other aunt nodded in approval. I heard Sonny's voice, and Holland smiled and headed into the parlor, where he had promised to play moody room with Sonny and Buzz. The women were left alone.

"I'm happy for you, too, Alice," I said.

Alice smiled and nodded her head; she hadn't said a single word about the marriage since the announcement.

"We're all very happy for her," her sister said, in plain contradiction of her manner. "Here's your present, Pearlie, a bit early I know." It was a simple silver box, containing an expensive cosmetic. It was one of those lipsticks with a little oval "lip mirror" attached to the case; they were popular at the time.

"This must change things for you," I said as I brought out the lipstick, venturing again onto the topic of marriage. "You're so used to living together. Does your fiancé have a house, Alice?"

She nodded very faintly and quickly, the orchid bouncing on her breast.

"He has a house in Santa Rosa."

"But that's so far!" I said without a thought.

Both of their faces blanched immediately. "It's not that far," Beatrice said at last. "It's thirty minutes over the bridge."

I noticed, in the little lip mirror, a reflection of the men in the other room. Holland and Buzz seated on the rug beside each other, faces to the light. Sonny must have been posing in a corner, and their watchful eyes narrowed in concentration. I could not see what my son was doing; I could only see the men, and I watched as both their faces burst into delight. One man's hand went to the other's shoulder, for balance, and remained there.

"It's thirty minutes over the bridge," the eldest sister repeated. I realized this was going to be their line with everyone. "It's absolutely nothing; sometimes it takes me thirty minutes just to find Alice where we're living now!" They both giggled and I could see how they had been as girls.

It took a moment, looking at the two of them, before I understood the very real and terrible story they were trying to tell me. A life together, bound by some treaty signed long ago and now, suddenly, at the last moment, abandoned. Forsaken. All for an old love Alice had given over years before, the one that had left its mark on her, the married man. Long forgotten, surely, by her older sister. Who knows what spinster scene occurred in that old house on Fillmore, the cats silent as jurors on the sofa. I felt so sorry for the one left alone, grinning at me so graciously. So late in life, she had not expected this particular tragedy.

And the other: eyes darting around the room, orchid wilting on her breast, a Delphic smile.

From the front room, I heard my husband shouting: "Passion! Passion!"

"You look beautiful today," Buzz told me the next time we met at Playland, then looked me up and down. "You're wearing my present!"

The corselette had arrived by courier the day before, thunderhead gray, packed in red tissue like a steel-boned heart. "I . . . I'm getting used to it."

"It's a strange sensation, isn't it? Freeing, in a way."

I asked if he had seen them yet.

"Not yet. I was looking out at the ocean. But I heard they would be here."

I said, "I wonder if they even came at all . . ."

He produced a pair of field binoculars that he unfolded as tenderly as an entomologist spreads a moth's wings. Through these he began to scan the crowd for Annabel and her beau.

We walked down the boardwalk, Buzz and I, with the low fog blowing in veils around our shoulders. We watched the San Francisco characters go by: the gray-haired "gracious ladies" in long-sleeved prim flour-sack colors; the bulb-nosed salesman already three drinks into the day and smiling at everyone; the gangs of Irish boys bitterly walking around, hands in pockets; the girls in Dale Evans outfits; the sprinkling of Filipinos recently arrived and Americanizing themselves (every one of them, from grandfather to grandchild) by wearing the national headgear: Mickey Mouse ears. A Negro couple caught my eye in a moment of wary alliance.

"Air-raid drill! Prepare basement plan!" A newspaper boy, shouting the headlines to us: "Air-raid drill coming!"

"Do you think he'd marry her, if it came down to it?" Buzz asked.

"I wonder if *she* would marry *him*."

"Oh she's the marrying kind."

"You really think she matters? Removing her will make a difference?"

"I've thought about it a long time," he said, peering through the binoculars again.

"It isn't just for spite, Buzz?"

He kept scanning the crowd, adjusting the dial at the bridge. At last he said, "No. I hope I never become someone like that." His eyes snapped sideways. "There they are."

And there they were: at the very front of the roller coaster. It had just finished boarding and the announcer was telling them to prepare for the thrill of their lives. Young William was all grins, a quiet contentment becalming his snub-nosed face below his active eyebrows; he was dressed in a leather flight jacket, a tie, and a newsboy cap, which in a clever afterthought he snatched off his head and sat upon, goofily grimacing. Annabel was gay as ever in a nautical skirt and pearls. I noticed a pair of glasses tucked inside her breast pocket.

"Yep," Buzz said. "The marrying kind."

With a jolt they were off—Annabel nervously clutching William, charms all aglitter—and the car began its clicking ascent to the top. There weren't seat belts or guardrails or any of the contraptions we have today. All that stood between Annabel and William and their death was a flat metal grid at the front of the car and their feet wedged in tightly below it. And so it was possibly with real terror, and real delight at the act of conquering death, that as their car tipped past its no-turning-back-now point at the top and her hair was flattened by a blind rush of wind, Annabel screamed ecstatically and raised an arm in triumph and I could see her brash appeal, her bright metallic strength. Anyone would melt in the glow of that glorious face. Then the coaster was lost in blind turns and coils among the wickerwork of the ride.

Buzz said he had learned something about William. "From your neighbor Edith."

"You've been talking to Edith?" I asked. I was feeling slightly dizzy: the whirligig motion of the ride seemed to mirror the rush of my own blood.

"On the streetcar. I learned he's going on a trip next week. And that he's not been drafted because of a mistake," he said. "The army somehow got it into its head that his brother was a prisoner of war in Korea, and so when William went before the draft board they labeled him 4-G."

"Oh, the Sullivan boys." They were five brothers who had died together in the war. The country felt the grief so deeply that the government changed the draft so no mother would have to bear it again. Any boy whose father or brother had died in combat was exempt.

"He probably didn't question it. He's the kind of good young man who follows orders, and they told him to stay home and pray to his brother. That's what Edith said."

I said, "He doesn't have a brother."

"I know."

"He only has a nine-year-old sister, I've seen her at the park."

"Apparently it was a mix-up with names."

The unbelievable luck some people have. If Holland had gotten a deferral for such a simple mistake, it would have gone so differently. If a typewriter had jammed improperly in Washington, D.C.—giving him an imaginary brother—none of us might be here except Annabel and her boy. Holland would have stayed home with his mother, unbroken; Buzz would have had some other roommate, and some other love. But then there would have been no Holland trapped with me in a room, no whispered words, no kisses. I would have lost him anyway.

Buzz made a casual suggestion. I pulled a notepad from my purse and, silent as a secretary, took down his words exactly. It seemed as harmless and impossible as all the rest; the action one might take in a dream. Later that night, I transcribed his words on our basement typewriter with its sticky *T*, folding the letter and placing it in its envelope. But by then, as if waking from a trance, my doubts would return. So there it would lie for weeks, abandoned, on our basement shelf.

"What do you think?" Buzz asked me that day below the roller coaster. "Is it too cruel?"

"No," I said. "The war is over."

"A conchie and an accomplice, it doesn't seem right."

"Something might happen all on its own."

"You mean Holland might change," he said, frowning, and I read his mind: I was clinging to the past again, to fantasy. Holland had not changed from the minute he was dragged from the ocean, seaweed-striped. It was only my image of him that had changed, shifted in and out like a clumsily focusing lens. I understood from Buzz's frown that change was not something you waited for, quietly, mutely, in a house by the ocean; that nobody was going to change, not Holland or the aunts or Annabel, that nothing would ever change unless we forced it into shape.

"Those Selective Service mistakes are notorious," Buzz said, looking out to sea. "They sent a CO like me out to a hospital of army boys."

"And roomed you with a Negro."

He nodded. "He wasn't too popular there, I'm sure he's told you. We were both so despised." Then, out of nowhere, Buzz asked me if I thought he was a coward.

"Well, I think William hasn't even—"

"I mean me."

He said it very calmly; he was used to people calling him a coward. Later, he would mention hitchhiking his way into town, when he would be stopped by cops who wondered why he wasn't in uniform—boys his age were all in the army—and who, after seeing his CO armband, would drive off into the gloom as if they had met a ghost. Either that, or aim a gun until he ran off himself.

"To tell the truth I'm not sure," I said. "I don't understand you, that's all."

"You said you weren't ashamed of your husband for hiding from war. I wonder what you think of me."

"Why did you do it?" I asked.

"It made sense to me. I didn't want to kill, I couldn't do it. I did a lot of reading, a lot of thinking about it. It seemed to me that it was what made us human. Deciding not to kill."

I asked if he just refused to go.

"No, no," he said, pausing. I expected him to be embarrassed, to balk at my asking him, but I saw something sharp appear in his eye. There was a reason he was telling me this story, but I didn't understand it then. "I was actually called for induction in 1943 and I went."

"What happened?"

"It was at a local school done up as a draft center. And we had to take off our clothes and stand around with all the other men, going from one doctor to another before they approved us and sent us on to a smaller room. We had to dress and stand in rows, waiting for an officer to arrive. I'd heard about that moment," he said, holding my gaze. "I'd heard a moment would come when the officer would walk into the room, ask us to say the oath, and then to take one step forward to become a soldier."

"That's how it's done?" He nodded. It seemed so Roman to have your life decided by a purely symbolic act, but I suppose that's how life is decided fairly regularly.

"I didn't take that step forward," he told me. "All the others did, they all said the oath and stepped forward. But not me. So they yelled at me for an hour and sent me to a psychiatrist. They were pretty hard on me." But he wouldn't budge. Young men are made of the strangest stuff. He said they registered him 4-E and gave him an armband. Yellow, of course—he laughed.

"And they sent you away? To the camps?"

"Oh yes."

"Did they hurt you?"

"No," he said, very far away now. "They didn't need to. We did that on our own."

I wanted to ask what he meant, but I saw the sharp, clever look leave his eyes. Instead, in an automatic action he would have prevented if he could, his right hand went out to rub the stump of his little finger, to soothe it like an injured child; it was his "tell," as they say in poker parlors. It was the sign of some private pain that had nothing to do with Holland, or me, and yet might explain what had brought Buzz Drumer here.

He chose not to go to jail, he told me. Selective Service offered other tasks an objector could still do for his country, including pulling stumps in a northern state, and that is what he did.

How would you picture a camp for conscientious objectors back in 1943? Perhaps as a traveling tent show: a caravan of white dormitories, a great gold big-top. The word "camp" brings to mind swimming, painting, races; most Americans pictured it that way, full of cowards and traitors and spies having a wonderful time. But what Buzz saw, as he arrived by car down a muddy road, was an internment camp.

It was run by the Quaker church "in the spirit of individual pacifism," but they in turn took their orders from Selective Service, which reluctantly accepted the camps only as a way to keep these abnormal men imprisoned, working without pay for the duration of the war. Buzz had no idea. "You can bunk with the Quakers, the Catholics, or the Coughlinites," he was told.

He'd had a fantasy they would all be like him: misfits, pacifists, outsiders. He picked the Quakers out of instinct; he was raised Baptist, and the only other Baptist was a colored man who played the cello, and lived with the Quakers. There was only one colored man in the whole place, and only one Jew.

The Jew was a problem for the Coughlinites. They were the followers of Father Charles E. Coughlin, a Detroit radio priest who felt America should not be fighting against that hero of the twentieth century: Adolf Hitler. These men weren't pacifists at all. How had they convinced the draft board? Perhaps some psychologist had nodded his head at their ideas and stamped their forms out of unimaginable sympathy. And so there they were, living under a president they saw as a Jewish conspirator. The Coughlinites were loathed by their fellow Catholics, who hated them nearly as much as the do-gooder Quakers.

So the Jew had to be kept away from the Coughlinites, who had to be kept away from the other Catholics, who had to be kept away from the Quakers. The colored man had to be kept away from everybody. In a pacifist camp. Those were the times we lived in.

"It was a dull, strange kind of life," Buzz said.

The day began with the yelling of the night watchman to head to the work trucks. Work was pulling stumps from a field, and Buzz's job was to coil the chain around the stump before another man turned on the winch to haul it away. The only satisfying moment of the day came when that stump would pop out, like a rotten tooth, and a secret hell of worms and Paleolithic beetles would gape before them. The stumps were chopped up into firewood, and stacked in a long wall in the woods, where they rotted all through the war; nobody used them. The field was never plowed. It was the kind of work you imagine angels devising for uncertain souls, endlessly raking the clouds.

Men went insane from the monotony, the wormy sky, and the wormy oatmeal, but mostly they went insane from the sense that they did not matter. The earth was burning itself to the ground, east and west of America, and they took no part in it. It drove some men to go AWOL, and some to join the army and go to war, or to sail away and die out on an ocean. Many others, including Buzz, sought another way out. It is surprising, he said, to learn that a man needs to matter.

A chorus of screams silenced Buzz's story; the ride had come to an end. Buzz crossed his arms and looked away. I wanted to say something to him, but the noise overwhelmed any talk, so we merely stood and watched them together: William laughing with just his top teeth showing, eyes hidden under the shadows of his thick eyebrows, arm now around his girl (it must have happened at a turn in the track), and Annabel slumped in hysterical false terror beside him.

"Take your girl to the Limbo ride!" the barker beside us comically cried.

"Yes," said Buzz quietly. "She's the marrying kind."

As the operator let them out of the gate, Annabel stumbled and grasped at William for support, holding his right arm, laughing, for once forgetting the cares of her father, her future. No one could ever wish her harm.

"Come see Limbo!"

∽

It happened the day the dog ran away. Sonny was staying with the aunts at their house on Fillmore, Lyle was out in the backyard, and I came home to find Holland in the living room, reading. It was very still and quiet, as it often was in the Sunset; all one heard was a soft burring noise that sounded like a warplane nosing its way through the clouds but was just someone mowing his lawn.

"Pearlie," Holland said to me as I walked in and set my purse on the console.

"Yes?"

I heard him say he wanted to tell me something.

"Hmm?" I said absently, looking for my keys.

I heard a low tremor in his voice: "There's something I haven't asked you."

"What is it?"

"I'm not much of a talker," he said plainly. "But I needed to ask you. I . . ."

He was staring at me. His book lay open beside him on the couch, one page stretching out into the air and slowly falling over as it lost his place. I turned my body to face Holland completely—my listening posture—and his face was as square and golden as an idol's, his eyes bright, his striped shirt undone beneath his cardigan, one button dangling from its unraveling thread. He sat and planned his words. What a strange, sad thing to be a man. How awful to be beaten by life as much as anyone and yet never be allowed to mention how it feels. To sit in your home that you have paid for with your labor, beside a wife who knows your youthful secrets; to have traveled around the world to escape the prejudices

of home and find them, now merely whispered, in the neighborhood around you; to have the past knock on your door in the
form of Buzz Drumer. I cannot envy men their silences.

"Holland, what is it?" I asked almost in a whisper.

But I will have to imagine forever what it was, because an in-
human sound suddenly flooded the room. The air-raid drill.

"What do we do?" my husband asked, looking around him.
The siren roared like a beast that had not been fed.

"We secure the windows," I shouted. "We turn off the appli-
ances and we wait in the shelter." I was glad to be an expert. "Secure the windows, that means—"

"I know how to secure a window," said the proud military
man, and he went to the front room, latching things and pulling
the blinds, as quick as a seaman, so I went around the kitchen and
unplugged everything I could think of, grabbing the radio as I
went. "Lyle, Lyle!" I yelled, but he was off somewhere and
couldn't hear me; there was no time to go and fetch him. Cars
stopped all over the city; Market Street became a long parking lot
as people huddled down during the drill; and everywhere people
were running inside their houses, pulling out their newspapers,
trying to remember what to do if the earth caught fire.

"The basement," I said loudly. He nodded and followed me. I
shouted for him to watch his step, there was a tricky drop at the
end, and I was, after all, so used to caring for his health. He said
nothing but simply put two fingers lightly on my shoulder. Down
we went into the darkness; it was the opposite of Orpheus.

We waited on a cot beneath the naked bulbs of the basement,
their filaments shivering like the husks of insects. The alarm sang
like a buzz saw over everything: the train set with its town and
trees and mirror lake, whose tiny abandoned boat always made
me imagine a hungry local sea monster. The shelves of our belongings: an old oil-gleaming pistol (beside it, its lover: a bullet),
pens, stationery, and stamps, and one particular envelope.

"What were you going to ask me?" I tried to say over the alarm.

"What?"

"You wanted to ask me something, before—"

"Oh nothing nothing just . . . I wanted to . . ."

Down in the basement, the siren spun in our ears like a top. Holland took off his sweater; I unbuttoned my top button; we were just a few feet from the furnace.

And then, all of a sudden, the noise stopped. What a cool, crisp silence we sat in.

"We've got to wait for the all clear," I said at last.

The moment for his speech had passed, but he stared at me as if I were the great mystery of the ages instead of the wife he had lived beside all these years. I looked away uncomfortably. I realized I did not want to hear whatever he'd been trying to ask me. The cowardly part of me wanted him to do the honorable thing; to come to his senses, silently and bravely.

I said, a little loudly, "I hope Lyle's not frightened."

He looked worried. "I forgot to warn Sonny about the air raid."

"I'm sure the aunts told him," I said.

"I just forgot all about it."

"It's okay. I'm sure they didn't forget, they read the paper."

He laughed at that. "I guess they do."

"He'll be good."

He smiled and said, "I haven't been down here in a while. It's so quiet and dark."

"It is."

"It reminds me of my mother's house," he said. "The smell of a closed-up room. I can't believe you visited me all the time. I can't believe they never caught you."

"Your mother was the clever one."

Holland leaned toward me and the old lightbulbs shivered. He said, "Why didn't we ever do more than kiss?"

The strange quiet of the basement took me back to his dark room in Kentucky, Holland's younger face staring at me with an expression of either gratitude or desire. Maybe, for him, there was no difference between the two.

"You were the only girl I saw for six months," he said, shaking his head. "You know that's all I dreamed of after a while? The shades, the bunk bed, the poetry you read to me. And Miss Pearlie."

He had never called me that before. A phantom girl haunting him at night, just as he haunted me for all the months of his imprisonment, the years without him and of course the years with him, sleeping in his bed behind that door. In dreams, he came to me with wide arms, promising things a waking Holland could never deliver. He told me everything then, meant all of it, opened his spectral chest to display for me—his beating transposed heart. He swore he loved me. But I had never thought that he had dreamed of me, back in those dim-lit days of war. How beautiful to find you once were someone's ghost.

His face searching mine for the answer to an unasked question—it belonged to the imprisoned boy in that room when I came one winter's day to find him standing in the bright light of an open window. "Holland, you'll be seen!" I had whispered. I ran to pull the shade, and when I turned around, I saw him. Tall and skinny, underfed, clothes hanging from him. He had the look of those fire-stricken buildings that are beautifully painted on the outside and only show, at the smoke-scarred windows, where the fire has burned everything inside. I was too young to know about internment, how it bends the mind.

As we waited in that basement for the all clear, another window opened in my mind, another Holland in another room. The look in Buzz's eyes as he awakened; it could not have been too different from Holland's that snowy day in Kentucky. A burned-out face trying not to break open at the horror he has seen. The way they look at you, those poor broken men; it's not empty or terrified at all. It's as if you were the first sign of life, of beauty, after a long, long winter. Does love always form, like a pearl, around these hardened bits of life?

"I'm sorry I never wrote," he said.

"I can't possibly understand what you went through."

He nodded, looking at his father's gun on the shelf. "But I'm sorry all the same. And we never got to say goodbye."

I shrugged. "I didn't know if I'd ever see you again."

"I can't possibly understand what you went through."

I shivered, despite the heat of that basement. "Well we survived it, didn't we?"

"We sure did," he said, grinning. "You and me and Countee Cullen."

I could see in his eyes that he wanted to say something more, perhaps try at last to make things right. The sad smile, the sorry shake of his head. The attempt, this time, to say goodbye.

I felt my husband's hand on my shoulder.

He whispered close: "I have a rendezvous with life . . ."

I looked up, and there he was smiling at me, his shirt unbuttoned, revealing a dark triangle of skin.

The small dark room when we were young. A boy in his hot summer bed, dreaming of me; a boy gone a little mad. And when he whispered, "Pearlie, is this what you—" I guessed his question, and I let him. I took it as a token, as if in a time of war; a wordless way to say goodbye. There on the cot with the train village below us. There with the long wait for the all clear, an answer to both our questions that day. As he caressed and kissed me, we could hear the low movements of the wind as it stepped up to the house, and over it, around it, making the beams creak ever so slightly like a hospital patient shifting in his bed. For a moment, we were our younger selves.

We think we know them, the ones we love—for can't we see right through them? Can't we see their lungs and organs hanging like grapes under glass; their hearts pulsing right on cue; their brains flashing with thoughts we can so easily predict? But I could not predict my husband. Every time I thought at last I'd seen to the bottom of him—he clouded over.

For, just as he was undoing my buttons to reveal Buzz's present, that corselette as spring-loaded as my heart, he said something that stopped me.

I pulled my blouse together and moved away. "What did you say?"

He sat up slightly. "I said, 'Don't ever change.'" There was that smile.

Don't ever change: I felt a part of my mind burst into flame. For change was all that was called for; change was the only item on the menu. There was no other possibility, and yet here he stood and, smiling like a boy, commanded me never to change. Here at last I had thought he'd submitted to his life and was telling me so, in his quiet way. That he longed for change: for who could endure our lives as they were? I was prepared to give him what he wanted, if he would choose it. If, like the rest of us stepping toward the edge of thirty, he would figure out at last his heart's desire.

"I'm too tired," I said, sliding out from under him.

"Oh," he said, surprised. I'm not sure anyone had ever stopped that handsome man from kissing them.

He looked at me expectantly, but I couldn't say anything. If I tried to open my mouth there wouldn't be an atom of oxygen in the room. The gun's eye winked in the darkness. No. He was never going to change.

Of course he wasn't. Why had I ever thought he might? It was not even possible; he was a fog that cannot change because it has not fixed a form. He was so used to being all things, pleasing all people. *Yes, yes, of course*, I imagined him whispering to Buzz, enjoying the odd flush on that man's cheeks, never meaning a word of it. No, to change anything could only mean mortal danger— could only mean losing the ones who adored him, losing his wife or son, losing his own sanity if anyone strayed an inch from where they stood. No, nothing was going to change; he would bask in the admiration of an old lover, a young girl, his bewildered wife, who knows who else—this would go on forever until he was arrested or blackmailed or worse.

Then it came. The all clear—the hopeful, singing note of it—
and in the instant afterward, we could hear neighbors yelling after our dog.

"Are they calling Lyle?" I asked, standing up.

"I guess so—"

"Do you think he got out under the fence? We should have
fixed that hole."

Holland looked very worried. "He can't survive out there
alone, he can't even bark. Poor old thing."

"Sorry?"

"I said he'll never survive out there alone. He ain't the kind."

Those words shot like darts across the room. "Am I the kind?"

"What are you talking about?"

"Wait there."

"What are you doing, Pearlie?"

I took what I needed from the shelf and held it in my hand.
And then, as he looked at me with the tender bemusement of a
husband, I decided to do what was necessary.

A moment later, I walked upstairs, out through the back door
and into the garden, draped with vines. A crowd of untended roses
lay bruised and blue in the dusk, alongside daylilies caught in the
act of closing for the night. In one, a tardy bee engrossed herself
among the shutting petals. Perhaps she would linger too late, become trapped in the mindless flower, struggling in there all night
long, exhausting herself to death in that pollened room.

Holland was already in the street calling the dog's name. He
was crouched down, clapping his hands and yelling: *"Come boy!
Lyle! Come boy!"* He suggested walking to the ocean; it seemed
like a place a mute dog might go, and so we went down Taravel
to where the twilight sky opened up above us, packed with clouds
and pink as a tongue. There I dropped an envelope into the little
iron mailbox on the corner. And then, his face toward an ocean

my ancestors had never crossed, a blameless ocean, his back to a country that did not love us, Holland sighed and looked at me, his eyes as trusting as ever.

I didn't touch that gun on the shelf. Of course not; I am no murderess. It lay in the basement, as quiet as ever, deep in its long-deserved sleep from another war. And yet, though no one heard it, from that mailbox down on Taravel a silent bullet was already headed for its target.

A month after the air-raid drill, the fog released its hold over the city and the sun began to reach as far as the Panhandle, and then to Kezar Stadium, and then at last into the Outside Lands. San Francisco isn't a city for the twentieth century; its persistent cool is meant for women in horsehair crinolines and men in wool frock coats, not for a modern show of neck and leg. So all of us were out, taking advantage of the sun and warmth like children taking advantage of a parent's jolly mood, and some of those days, walking with Sonny out by the ocean, I found myself imagining Lyle.

Who knows what voice whispers nightly to an animal until, driven mad by the air raid, he digs at the sandy dirt of our backyard and wriggles until he is free. Where would he go? To the ocean, I imagined. Every scent, every track must lead down to the ocean.

I imagined him running across the Great Highway with its rumbling trucks, onto the sand of the Pacific. Straight into the water itself—his breed had a love of water—wrestling aimlessly with the foam, tongue flapping, instinct telling him there was something to be done here. And, once done, he could come home. But for some magnificent reason he had forgotten home— he had forgotten me and Holland and his best friend Sonny, his allies (the bowl and the leash and a series of blue rubber balls), his enemies (the postman, the train set, the demonic black telephone)—and now was out in the world without a compass.

Golden Gate Park—surely that's where he headed next. Into the tulip garden, where tourists dropped half-eaten egg-salad sandwiches, to the golf course with trails of spilled whiskey, in a loping run he crossed it with the wind in his ears and only a far-off trio of men to watch him, as the golden streak of him passed across the green, grinning as dogs grin, all memory of us utterly erased. All memory of shoes and socks and shameful errors on the carpet. Past squirrels in the park, fussing like accountants, and blue herons imitating statues in a muddy pond, and once in a while a hawk flying overhead, eye trained on a hapless mouse. Maybe trained on Lyle. Perhaps house cats, having slipped their keepers, lay hidden in the rhododendrons, and lizards and snakes and rabbits; perhaps whole colonies of them existed, burrowed deep under the lawn-bowling courts, or hiding all day in the Tea Garden and emerging at night to eat the remains of crumbled tea crackers. Pets, beloved, cosseted, having broken their chains, wandering the Outside Lands. Living together, wild, in the park, hunting in packs beneath a waxing moon. Some accidental frequency in the siren had lit a gene like a flare in their rib cages, freeing them—for what greater freedom could there be than to forget your home?

Buzz was out of town for a week, and the news was almost entirely taken up by the last throes of the war and by the approaching execution of the Rosenbergs. Their final Supreme Court appeal was sure to be denied and it seemed a foregone conclusion that they were going to die. I remember very clearly an image of Eisenhower (who refused them clemency) smiling broadly and how some newspaper artist had replaced each of his teeth with a tiny electric chair. But there wasn't a single person in my neighborhood who doubted the Rosenbergs' guilt, doubted that they had a console table made for photographing documents instead of one bought at Macy's to hold the telephone, or doubted the system of justice that had tried and convicted them, or the highest court that would never hear their appeal. So the conversations in the Sunset weren't arguments for or against execution—that talk was going on east of us, in North Beach, or even among the colored Communists out on Fillmore, none of whom we knew—no, our part of town experienced the dawn excitement of a mob, each of whom had brought a picnic for the hanging.

When we met again at Playland, I told Buzz I'd done what he'd asked. He seemed startled—a spasm of conscience—then put his hat on the seawall and said, "I'm sure it's too late." I said it was all I could think of to do. "Don't worry, we'll see what happens." Surely nothing would come of it. Birds by the dozens were sitting on the sand and staring at us, chirping. We stood for a long time by the seawall, camouflaged by passing crowds, with nothing to say to each other. It was when we left the boardwalk that we were almost caught.

Buzz was discussing our next rendezvous—he had a movie theater in mind—as we stood beside that Limbo ride, about to be consumed by a crowd of popcorn-eating Boy Scouts. He was leaning very close to me so he could be heard above the boys tomahawking the air, when I saw two familiar straw hats with fluted ribbons emerge from the park.

"Pearlie!" they cried.

I immediately stepped sideways and let Buzz be swallowed by the Scouts (popcorn eruption, "Hey there, mister!"), and I kept moving until I faced the aunts alone.

"You've gone out for a walk!" one announced.

I said, "Edith is looking after Sonny."

Another looked at me carefully. "Is Holland here?"

"No, he's at work of course."

"Then what are you doing with his hat?"

I looked down and there it was, Buzz's two-ounce Dobbs that he was so proud of rolling up into his pocket and pulling out again unscathed; I must have picked it up off the seawall. A man's felt hat in my hand. I could not think of a single plausible explanation. But people are not as interested in us as we think they are. And so they did not blink an eye when I answered, "I have no good explanation."

"Well we heard the most terrible news," said Beatrice.

I smiled. Buzz stood hidden among the boys like a figure in a burbling fountain. "You don't say."

"There was a jealous wife. In Fresno."

"Didn't the last story happen in Fresno?" I asked.

"Well that is apparently where these things happen!" she told me, indignant. "A jealous wife borrowed a plane and crashed it into the playground near her house. And there was a note."

"Listen to this," said Alice, wearing the glow of old love like a veil. "There was a note for her husband that said: 'You told me once that everyone gets over everything. But it isn't true and I'll prove it.' Imagine writing a thing like that."

"I certainly can't."

"And to prove it, she took away the things he loved," Beatrice said.

Her sister repeated: "The things he loved—"

Beatrice sniffled. "Only the awful part is, the awful part—"

The awful part was that their daughter had been in the plane, and the family dog as well; the things he loved. They had all gone down together in a flower of flame. It was not a radio show, this time.

One aunt was sighing: "That husband, to watch that plane go down—"

"That's jealousy for you," the other said and looked at me very meaningfully. "That's what women are capable of. When in most marriages, you know, they can work these things out." She stood there like a stone column, repeating: "Most couples can just work these things out."

"How awful," I said, "what a thing to think about before your wedding, Alice."

"Well—" she began.

"And you know that friend of Holland's, that nice white fellow," her sister broke in. "Well I don't want to spoil your friendship. But you should know that he's a liar. A notorious liar."

"Oh yes, Pearlie," Alice said, nodding.

"He tells people he was an objector. But he wasn't. He was a coward. A coward and a liar. He cut off his finger to get out of the fighting, oh yes he did, you can see it right there."

"We wouldn't have much more to do with him, if we were you."

"Think of Sonny."

I wonder what those women were up to. They must have known a great deal more than they were letting on. The lunch long ago, the "worry over the past" and the one's cry—"Don't marry him!"—made it clear they were paying attention. They could feel something changing, as the blind can sense a storm, and were working in their fumbling manner to stop us. In some terrified way, they were trying to help me.

It was only much later that I realized they must have seen to the marrow of everyone involved. They had spent their spinster hours knitting away in front of us, that generation of women who listened to nothing but watched everything, and they had seen our hearts' desires. I am not saying they approved of them. I think those two women cared only to keep their nephew happy, or what they viewed as happy, and they would have done anything to save him. They had thought that I would save him, but they had begun to doubt. I hadn't the instinct. I was the type that saw nothing, and then saw everything. I think to save someone, you have to be like the aunts, and look at life with half-closed eyes, and never waver. Yes, I think the key to that kind of life is never to waver.

The aunts handed me a gift for Sonny, a pretty pink little box, and said they'd be by at two, they could hardly think properly they were so upset, they might treat themselves to sukiyaki, and off they went like two beach balls rolling along the sidewalk, one in polka dots, one in stripes, smiling at each other. Sweet old cats, their conjoined life about to come to its end; the last of their mutual meddling.

I opened the box. It was a trio of knitted hand puppets: a tiger, a judge, and a wizard. I smiled and studied the beautiful things; they must have chosen these puppets so carefully from the shop, picked among the flawed handmade toys, and yet what scenario these three could enact together was a puzzle. A tiger, a judge, and a wizard . . . some nightmare divorce proceeding? And did they consider my Sonny a three-armed Martian?

"I'll take my hat now, madam, thank you."

Buzz smiled as he brushed popcorn from his sleeves. He led me out through the crowd and my heart fell back into its normal rhythm. He took my arm again and whispered, "The way you acted, you'd think *we* were the lovers . . ."

Two weeks later it happened at last; they printed his name on the page beside Weddings and Divorces:

Drafted: William Platt, Sunset District . . .

Annabel DeLawn married William Platt on May 20, 1953, after only a week's engagement; it happened more quickly than we'd ever expected. The ceremony was a small one at Yosemite Hall, attended by the surviving members of her father's army regiment. I clipped the photo out of the paper. He was in his army uniform. And she was in a plain white dress with a long piece of lace over her head, the way my mother would lay a dish towel on a freshly baked pie to keep off flies. "The beautiful daughter of General DeLawn," read the caption, and I had to agree. It was only the day after William Platt's name appeared in the newspaper, on the draft rolls, that she announced she was going to marry him, though of course she didn't have to. And it wasn't in order to save him from the war; there was no exemption left for William Platt, and she wasn't the type to hide a man from battle, anyway. Very few of us are that type. No, Annabel married William the Seltzer Boy—as I knew she would—because she loved him.

"I didn't even know they were engaged," Holland said as I showed him the announcement in the paper. He undid the noose-knot of his tie. His eyes revealed nothing.

"I guess they kept it secret. And then William got drafted, so the secret came out."

He folded the tie around his hand. He said he remembered lots of boys getting married before they were shipped out.

"I remember that, too." I didn't mention it was for deferrals.

It was sure rotten to get drafted, he said, and gave a sad smile. If there was a last scene with Annabel, on a cliff by the roaring ocean, a grimace of canceled desire, some tearless goodbye—"I guess I'm going to be a good wife"—then he did not show it. No ice clinked in his bourbon; his hand was steady as ever.

"He'll be fine. They're just training them these days, they won't even ship him out." He nodded and looked right at me. We did not speak, that day, of how a boy might hide from war.

No one ever wondered why William's luck broke in the end. The notice just arrived one morning and the family acted as if it was the summons they had always expected, the fulfillment of some prophecy; there was no drama about it at all. The war was nearly over. Our president promised us: the mission was almost complete, and we had no reason to disbelieve him. He was, after all, a general. One last push and it would be finished; certainly no newly drafted troops would be sent. The joke at the wedding (among the ancient army men) was that William would not even get to sample Korean "cooking" (said with a filthy gesture) before he came home to good old American potatoes. Apparently William looked around, grinning; I don't think he understood what they were talking about.

The end of the war. Buzz hoped it had come; that was the only way he could dictate that letter, back at Playland, with a clean conscience, though afterward, it seemed to us both like a heartless plan. So I hid it in the basement until the air raid. That night, with the siren still singing in my skull, I pulled it from the shelf and mailed it. I assumed nothing would happen; I believed our president, and thought of Korea as being as safe as Minnesota. It seemed blandly American to write a letter to the government: "It might interest Selective Service to know about a misunderstanding that an eligible young man has a brother . . ."

Signed with a slipknot *P* and posted by the ocean. Be a finker for Mr. Pinker.

❧

The cruelest part, to me, was not that we had sent William off to train for war. He was an average boy, with the average urges, prejudices, and habits; a more heartless person would find it poetic for him to stand in a long line of average boys and do what he was told. He had no idea why anyone would not step forward after the oath and become a soldier. I'm sure he believed it was for the common good, and perhaps it was. The disruption of his life, his happiness, his delivery route was a hardship he may not have deserved. But what haunted me was Annabel.

Marriage is a fairy tale, and, like those stories, it requires a bewitching bargain. It is to trade the thing you value most. In this one, she exchanged her future: Annabel Platt no longer went to State, no longer sat in sulfur-smelling classrooms with boys snickering beside her as the chalk scratched on the board, no longer smiled and removed a professor's hand from her thigh. There would be no more books for Annabel, no laboratory, no miracu-

lous discovery glowing in an Erlenmeyer flask. She had pawned
them all for him.

Her marriage: I had forced it, like a flower out of season. In my
air-raid panic, I had hastily executed Buzz's aborted plan and
never thought, for a moment, of any danger except to that young
man. Annabel's attentions to my husband were thwarted, but I
had never meant to thwart her life. She did that to herself, but
I can hardly blame her. Those were the times, the rules we lived
by. How devastating to remember that daydream of mine, seeing
her golden head in the soda shop, that brief murderous image. Of
course it was no more absurd than fantasies people indulged in
daily on the bus, the beach, about less-deserving subjects; I am
no murderess. If I could have found her once again in the soda
shop; if I could have crossed Mr. Hussey's race line to sit across
from her in that green-striped booth. If I could have explained
it all, perhaps she would have understood. But there was no way
to cross that line. So in the end, like a hunted creature trying to
throw the scent, I had freed myself only by shifting my fate onto
another woman.

During the war, cars had their chrome painted over, so our free-
ways wouldn't shine in the sun and make an easy target for the
Japanese. We grew so used to this dimness that it was a shock to
see something as ablaze as the expensive car that drove up to our
house. The sound of a horn brought me to the window, where I
saw it gleaming even in the dull Sunset sun, decorated everywhere
with bright chrome that made it seem so new. Everywhere down
the block, I saw housewives pushing lace curtains aside to stare,
and boys on bikes stopped on the sidewalk to look back, squinting, as from this car—bloodred, as huge and round as the belly of
a whale—stepped my private Jonah.

I walked outside, wiping my hands on a dishrag.

"Do you like it?" Buzz asked, grinning.

"Where did you get that?" I whispered, urging him into the house, but he stood outside, looking at the candied shine of the thing. He had become a little reckless, perhaps savoring this story that seemed so rapidly to be coming to its end.

He ran a hand along the swell below the window. "The dealer let me take it for a ride. Should I get it?" he asked. "It's really your money I'm spending, but I thought we'd leave you with the old Plymouth if you don't mind—"

I saw the wives at the windows and gestured to Buzz. "Hush, get inside."

"No, get Sonny," he said, opening the door. "Let's go for a ride."

I'm sure Sonny was the envy of the block as the other boys watched him climb into the front seat of that lovely car. He sat there at the wheel as if at the helm of a spaceship, his face wide open with pleasure, as he delicately touched, without pressing, every button he could find. I had him move over and I climbed into the passenger side. The door shut with a final sound.

"It's beautiful," I said to Buzz, who took over the driver's side. "I've never been in a car like this."

He looked very carefully at me, still smiling. "You like it? You can get a car like this, if you want to."

I glanced at the dashboard, the wheel, shaking my head. "No. But it's beautiful."

Buzz pushed his hat back on his head and started up the car. He said, "We'll need something nice and big to cross the country in." And for the first time in a while, the "we" he spoke of didn't include me.

I looked down at my son, then spoke softly to Buzz: "You're crossing the country? You've talked with him?"

"Just about me. Not about everything."

"I'd never know—"

"Later," Buzz said, his hand on Sonny's head. "I have something I want to show you."

I looked back at my married home. The old Cook home within the new development. White, square, a plain façade punctured by a ruby-colored section of glass above the doorway: cherry on a sundae. Overgrown with vines, of course, and handsome the way a domesticated animal is handsome: the house where every real event of my life took place.

The car started up with the low rumbling of a caged beast, and I sat and caressed its striped leather, imagining how its shiny newness would be coated in dust and crumpled bits of paper, crosswords and broadsheets; how in this same seat my husband might fall asleep for hot Nebraska hours while Buzz, the boss, drove a road so straight and empty he could read from a paperback novel propped up beside the dashboard. Across the Golden Gate, the property was greener than before, fooled by a lush out-of-season rainstorm, and seemed fuller in its thick coat of grass. I listened to Sonny shouting about his day from the backseat, my eyelids flickering with exhaustion, and I found myself staring sleepily out at the fog unrolling above us like fleece until my eyes closed.

I dreamed of William Platt, of all people. I dreamed that he was helping me over a wall, that it was very important we get over that wall because something was coming behind us—more than an enemy, of course—a monster, a darkness moving on the horizon. But I was caught in that dream substance that glues you to the spot; it kept me in danger as William pulled and pulled on my arm and called me a horrible name . . . and then suddenly we were in Playland, and I was sitting in the ride operator's seat, and William was on the ride itself—in a swan boat, for some reason, and not a hearse car—there he was, waving and waving at me with that broad smile as his boat approached the darkness. And then, like a movie shown with a missing reel, he was gone and standing before me was a rain-soaked Holland with a single word on his lips . . .

I awoke, alone, in a dandelion heaven. My heart was beating

rapidly; I let out a plaintive sob. The car was parked beside a dirt road, which parted the gold grass like a comb through hair, and, among the dandelions (young blonds and old grays), I noticed casual bouquets of poppies that seemed to sparkle. It took me a moment to realize it wasn't light but crickets, everywhere, leaping. They lay stone-gray on the ground, until disturbed, and then they leaped into the air and exposed their underwings, which shone for a moment a bright Prussian blue. Why this flash of color? How could it ever help the bugs survive? There is no explaining beauty.

Through the window I saw Buzz, sitting on a blanket beside a fascinated Sonny. The sun made them both shade their eyes with their hands, like surveyors. My son was all smiles, and he didn't notice a common butterfly writing in the air above him.

My door made an old-fashioned slam.

"I agree, that's a wonderful idea," I heard Buzz say, gesturing to the ocean swell of hills. "What kind of house would you put there?"

My son considered this a moment. "A tree house!"

Buzz laughed. "Well there ain't that many trees. How about a house on stilts?"

"All right."

"Show me where."

But I had already grabbed Buzz by the arm and pulled him through the weeds back to the car, crickets leaping everywhere. He looked amazed, as if I were a stronger woman than he'd counted on, but I did not wait for him to speak before I whispered furiously:

"How dare you?"

"I wanted to show Sonny—"

"I know what you're doing. I'm no fool."

"Little boys like to dream, too."

"How dare you show my son these things? Show him all this."

I thrust my arms out at the open sky, the clouds as bright and crenellated as the grass below, all of it moving, rustling, in the strong wind that smelled of the ocean. My scarf blew all around me. "Asking him what kind of house he'd like, my God! Get him dreaming and then you'll take it away."

He took off his hat and said, quite calmly: "It's going to happen, Pearlie."

"Don't make him promises. Don't break his heart."

"It's going to happen. Now there's nothing standing in our way. We're going to make it happen, together."

"It's going to happen *my way*," I said. "If I get the money, *your* money, I'll do what I like."

He looked away from me smiling slightly despite my shouting. He said, "It's five hundred acres, like you said."

"What do you mean?"

"Like you told me. I just wanted you and Sonny to see it."

I held my mouth open but could think of nothing to say. A turkey buzzard flew high above us, so high it looked as pretty as a hawk, hovering, adjusting its wings, staggering in the hot blue sky. Five hundred acres with a fence all around.

"It's too soon," I told him firmly.

"No, Pearlie. You have to prepare. If you know what you want, you can have it, but you have to let go of your old life, and of Holland—"

"I don't like it," I snapped at him. It made me angrier than ever, somehow, that he'd tricked a dream out of me. That he'd listened, and thought it over, and drove us out to see it. "I don't like it. You buy my husband from me—"

"Now calm down."

But I would not calm down. My voice was very soft and firm: "You buy my husband from me like he's at auction. You break up our family—"

"Pearlie—"

My hand gestured to where my son had wanted his house on stilts. "It's an old story." He knew what I meant.

"That doesn't seem fair."

I nodded. "It's fair enough," I said, then headed to the car.

"I'm trying to be a friend."

I turned around. He squinted in the bright sun, hat in hand, his hair flying in blond strands all around. I smiled. "We ain't friends, Mr. Charles Drumer," I said. "We ain't friends. We're just in this together. We're just . . . what did you say to me once? We're just born at a bad time."

"I see."

Sonny lay splayed on the blanket, asleep in the sun. Beyond him, the dirt road disappeared into the golden fur of the hills, and I saw how a little depression seemed to flourish with dark reeds where a small lake must have hidden, and beyond that, there between two peaks, like a diamond, lay the bright hopeful blue of the sea.

"I heard what you did in the war," I said.

He looked at me; perhaps I'd said it too sharply. "Holland tell you?"

"No, I heard elsewhere," I said. "They said you weren't a conchie, not really. That you were a liar. And a coward, just like Holland. They said you cut off your own finger to get out of fighting."

He looked like a man staring at a puzzle before putting it together. He asked, "Is that what you heard? It was to get out of fighting?"

"That's right," I said.

"That's not true," he said, not quite to me but to the air. "I've never told anyone, not even Holland." Before us, a large striped rock jutted up out of a high green hill; the deep crevice the stream had made crossed our view in a long, jagged shape, though the stream itself was hidden; there was the shape of movement all around us, but nothing moved. The land sat as still as a cat.

"What I told you was the truth, Pearlie," he said at last. "Let's leave it at that. I was sent to a camp. It was a long time ago."

But I would not let it be: "You got out somehow. You came out here."

"I already told you what that hospital was."

"You're saying you weren't faking it."

He turned to me. "That I was crazy?"

"Yes."

Buzz stood with his hands on his hips, letting the wind blow his shirttails around his body. "In India I visited a temple where the monks lived on nothing but sunlight. I think they had broth once a day, but they said it was air and light. It brought them visions, they said. Took them away from the illusions of the world," he said. He was not making any sense. "Have you ever gone to the edge of your senses? Have you ever starved?"

I bristled. "My parents did their best. It was a hard time."

"I want you to know I went to that edge," he said. "I wasn't faking it. What happened in the war, what happened to all of us, that's what I'm trying to prevent. The kind of thing that sent me to that hospital, the loneliness of that. I don't know how else to explain it. I was starting to feel it again in that bachelor apartment, the one you made fun of, the one with just one burner and no way out. I thought I'd gotten over Holland, and years went by. And then I felt it again. I wouldn't do all of this, put you through everything, if I knew some other way."

"The camp made you . . ." I couldn't quite bring myself to say it made him mad.

"Not the camp," he said. "I found a way out of the camp."

❦

Two visiting doctors helped him escape. Like medicine men arriving at a Western town, one tall with a thin beard, the other short and smiling. One was from Spain. They came at the end of

a workday, with the sky spread out above them like a great skele-
tal bird, pinked by a dropped sun, and the weary Quaker official
announced they were looking for healthy volunteers for a medical
study. This happened now and then; some men volunteered to
wear lice-infested underwear to test insecticides; some ate feces to
study hepatitis; some lived for a month at zero degrees; all of this
was just to do something, be worth something in a world at war.
These particular doctors simply handed out a pamphlet that read:
Will You Starve That They Be Better Fed?

"Do you have the weak mind?" the Spanish one asked Buzz in
a cold metal room, and he shook his head. "Do you have the tired
heart?" and he shook his head. It seemed impossible that these
could be the requirements for the study, and Buzz understood
only later that it was the doctor's poor English.

Buzz left the camp, he told me, and traveled to Minnesota on
a train ride that baffled him: coeds barging through the dining car
in sweater sets, screaming with laughter, and after them plunged
college boys in dinkies; and stranger sights, such as the man sitting next to an enormous cello, and a man standing in between
the cars, rolling his cigarettes in a little plastic machine, who smiled
and offered one for free—a world of plenty, a city, in other words,
though in every station they passed, a reminder was plastered for
passengers to read: IS THIS TRIP NECESSARY? SAVE FUEL FOR OUR
BOYS; COMBINE TRIPS OR DO WITHOUT. But no one in Min-
neapolis seemed to be doing without, not compared to where
he'd come from.

The hygiene laboratory offices were at a university, in little
green fluorescent rooms, and it was there he met the other men
in the experiment. Immediately he began to judge the others on
how well he thought they would adjust. Later they all learned that
none of the first impressions meant anything, not a strong hand-
shake, or a confident grin, or a healthy appetite, or even appear-
ing to have suffered from hunger and poverty; no one could
possibly have predicted who would snap under the strain.

They lived in something like a dormitory, the walls painted the same lichen green as the laboratories, with a lounge where they smoked and read magazines, or studied for classes—for they were allowed to attend classes—and there were no locks on the doors, no guards. That part of CO life was over. It was November in Minnesota, but Buzz and the other men felt their freedom as the first sign of spring.

Not that they had much time; language classes took up twenty-five hours a week, with an idea they might later go overseas and aid in refugee camps. They were given all kinds of menial tasks—laundry and cutting potatoes, nothing as degrading as the camps—and Buzz took a course in business and another in literature. He had never seen the inside of a college classroom before. Worrying that he didn't belong there, he sat on the aisle in the back, so that if asked to do so he could leave quickly and without embarrassment. "It was strange," he said, "in the classrooms, to see young men so relaxed and free." They seemed to follow the war closely, and some dropped out to join the fight, but only a few seemed awkward about being alive and reading Chaucer while the world was burning. Buzz felt very apart from them.

As for the experiment, at first it was no effort at all. They had to walk twenty-two miles a week, two miles to the dining hall for meals, some treadmill just for testing, in addition to sports or ice-skating or other activities they were free to enjoy. And for a long time, they ate as much as any man would. Better food than at the camps, or least more varied food than Spam and apples every night. It was about three months before the doctors told them the control period was over and they would begin a new regimen. Buzz looked forward to that. Unable to kill a man, unable to survive the camps. Here he was at last able to do his part.

He had never known what hunger was; how could he? How could any of us, who claim to be "starving" an hour or two after breakfast? During the Depression and war rationing, we thought we knew hunger. But we didn't. For the boys in Minnesota, meals went down to eight and five o'clock, portioned meagerly from cabbage and potatoes to less than half what they were used to eating. This went on for one month, two months, six months. Each man's body devoured a quarter of itself.

There is a face all starving people share: the dull apathetic stare you might recognize from footage of Africa, or from people on the street, and after only two months Buzz had that stare. It is called "the mask of famine." It comes from facial muscles that have withered away. Some parts of the body tighten with thinness, like the arms and legs, and some sag, like the knees. The lungs begin to fail; the heart loses its voltage; the pulse begins to slow, although the blood itself thins out with the water the body hoards, who knows why? Getting dressed becomes difficult; opening a bottle of longed-for milk seems ironically impossible; even a book cannot be held open long enough to read it. He learned the difference, he told me, between the longing ache of hunger and the swift, sharp jab. Sometimes hunger goes on so long, invades the body so deeply for its hidden stores that it gives a prophecy of old age; the spine collapses, the posture topples. A starving man of twenty might experience a sensation that he will not regain for sixty years: the feeling of having grown old. I wondered if Buzz would feel it again when real age came upon him, if one morning at eighty he would step out of bed and recall, with surprise, this same bone-creaking, shivering feeling—the body in old age—that he had felt before when he was young.

They stopped going to classes; they stopped ice-skating and exercises; they stopped everything but they couldn't stop dreaming of food, stealing menus from restaurants and going over each item like thieves planning a heist. Buzz's eyes became waxy and luminous, his spine as segmented as a larva, and his brain shifted in colored waves, an aurora borealis; he could no longer bear the treadmill, even for a few minutes, and not because he was too tired or lacked the will; he simply had no muscles left to move. He said he felt like a creature from a children's book, something unnatural: a kitchen broom brought to life. They told him his heart had shrunk to twenty percent of its normal size. It was the result of starvation, of course, but to his addled mind it made sense. "It came as a relief," he told me, for now how could anyone love him? And who could he ever love?

∾

"Everything all right here folks?"

A policeman leaned out of his patrol car, the window glass creasing his arm's under-fat. I suppose he was not used to seeing a white man, a colored boy and woman wandering the hills. He was talking to Buzz.

"Everything's fine, officer," the young man said very gently.

"This is private property, you know. You can't be trespassing here."

"I know the owner. We're potential buyers."

The policeman let that idea roll around in his skull like a gum-ball until at last, with a clank, it landed. He looked me over from top to bottom. "There's much nicer land elsewhere, for you folks," he said meaningfully, then advised us to move along. His exit conjured a genie cloud of dust.

I did not say a word. Rings of fear and rage were passing through me. Memories of Kentucky.

"It's late," Buzz said, hoisting his jacket onto his shoulder and approaching Sonny, who stirred one last time before letting his eyes flutter open. Buzz went over and picked the boy up in his arms, and my son feigned sleep as he always had with his father. The scenes of starvation hung around us in the air. Let him have it, I thought. What he wants is easy to give, and what I want I do not even know, though this will do. Five hundred acres with a fence all around. Let it end. The man carried the boy across the heaving, golden fur of the field and said, as he passed me, "We'll take your son back home." Let everyone have his wish.

❧

I had managed to save five thousand dollars from the allowances Buzz doled out, and without touching that nest egg I still had plenty to spend on Sonny. Buzz went on an extended trip—selling his factory, telling me to "sit tight and wait." I was glad to think about something other than the news of war and draftees. I bought Sonny new leg braces (the leather had worn out of the old ones), more doctor's visits, and, as a treat, secretly sponsored Hank, a neighborhood boy, in the Soap Box Derby with the agreement that Sonny could watch and help paint. The boy solemnly swore a complex Cub Scout oath, and we went together, the three of us, to a Chevrolet dealer on Van Ness to get the regulation racing wheels and parts for the car. For a week Sonny sat on a little stool and watched redheaded Hank nailing his car together, my son perfectly silent and still except the few times he asked a question ("Howzit steer?") and Hank raised his head with a long-suffering look and slowly explained.

I couldn't ever buy him Hank's kind of childhood, but I could make two dreams come true. One was to attend the races, where hay bales separated the onlookers from the racers themselves, some in helmets, most in baseball caps, floating down the hill in pinewood boxes painted in angry imitation of street-thug cars—flames, devils, snakes, thorns—though steered by angelic drivers. Hank came in near the back of the pack, but his loss allowed the second dream: folding up my son's weak legs into the car, teaching him to grip the wheel securely, and getting four reluctant boys to push him two blocks down a safe stretch of road. "Look at me!" he kept shouting. "Look at me!"

He told me, after it was over, that he'd won the race.

"Oh yeah, baby!" I said, lifting him out and laughing with him. "Yeah, baby, you won!"

While my son stared at Hank's car, I handed each freckled boy a dollar. But the rest I saved against our future, mine and Sonny's, no matter what happened. I could not give him their childhood, but I could give him this.

⌒

Usually, on a Saturday, Holland and I would drop by the Fursten-bergs to watch shows like *The Plainclothesman* and *Cavalcade of Stars* until we were too tired to see, and then we'd dream in a flicker of guns and singing Swedes. I was willing to keep our schedule, as I was willing to make his dinners and accept his kisses when he came home from work; my life was just a wait for this to end. So it surprised me, after dinner, when my husband suggested we go dancing.

"The Rose Bowl," he said.

"What made you think of that, after all this time?"

"It's Negro Night."

"I know." I took his plate, leaning toward the sink. "But that's so far . . ."

He looked up at me with his old grin. "Ain't you got a new dress to wear?"

There wasn't anyplace like the Rose Bowl—a dance floor built among the trees, their trunks rising through cutouts in the floor, their leaves loosely veiling the stars—no other place where a stinko soldier could lead his date smack into a sycamore and have to make up for it all night long. It lay across the bay, in Larkspur, and forty years earlier, young dancers used to take a ferry hung with sparkling lights, drinking from flasks, laughing as the boat dipped on the choppy water, tipsy as they were. The ferry was gone by 1953—the bridges had been put up—but when you drove out there you still felt part of something, and you would smile to see a car pull off at Larkspur, knowing it was some young man and his date. Sometimes they held a special night, like Cal Night or Veteran's Night, for white folks only. So on Negro Night we all came, old and young, out on that dance floor under the strings of fog-haloed lights, and the leaves falling down on you, and a huge paper moon someone had painted in our grandparents' day, winking at us like the very devil.

On the drive there, I realized how much time had passed since I'd been alone with Holland. I felt as an emigrant must, looking around the country she knows she must leave. We drove along and listened to the radio and he told me a story he'd heard at work: about a car accident, a blind woman whose dog was hit but who didn't realize her loss until a bystander told her. Then she leaned down and wept on the street. The kind of upsetting story I had always clipped from his papers.

"You think Sonny misses us?" I asked.

"I'm sure he does."

It was when he glanced over and grinned that I thought of what would soon be gone. The little hiccup that came and went in his conversations. His habit of easing his tired eyes by closing them tight and rolling them against his lids. Those silver-hat cuff links.

"You all right?" he asked me.

I said I was fine, and we should turn left at the light.

A handsome young man at the door took our money; beyond him, you could see the band, resting between sets and smoking cigarettes, joshing each other while a serious female saxophonist polished her instrument. The crowd was in a state of excitement as if a major dance number had just ended and they could have wept from joy; there was general chattering and laughing and a few young men kept dancing with their partners even without the music, eyes closed, unable to let go of a mood we'd arrived too late to catch. My husband yelled something at me I couldn't hear, then waved across the dance floor to a neatly mustached young soldier. They communicated in a wild semaphore, like mating birds, while I looked around the floor and saw the barkless tree trunks, polished by wallflowers' stroking hands, the clear sky pitted with stars above the garlands of lights that one young man was jokily reaching up to unscrew as his date beat him happily with her purse. The soldier arrived with glasses and a bottle, and I realized this was what Holland had been doing: getting us booze. He poured me one and I drank it down quick, then had another. The soldier offered us each a cigarette and in his smile I saw the crooked teeth of a boy born poor.

Holland introduced me to the young man (a former stock boy, now a private on leave) as "Mrs. Cook, who came here with me before we were married."

The young man brightened politely and asked if it had changed; as if it were so long ago.

"We only came here a few times," I said, not quite an answer.

"Hey, it's a good one!" Holland shouted and downed one drink, then another; he took our glasses and set them on a little stand, then grabbed me and began to spin me counterclockwise into the throng of couples.

Oh he could dance, my Holland Cook; he had excelled as a boy and now, without having been taught a thing, could look around and pick up steps, and my great talent was to follow. It's a trick young women these days can't possibly know: how to follow. One hand at your waist, the middle finger pressing, the other hand clutching yours, communicating in little spasms of delight, none of them rehearsed, some of them so unexpected you come out of a twirl and laugh—because there he is, grinning at you sideways in some move he's just filched from across the dance floor. He hadn't talent, exactly; like any dilettante, he invented nothing, perfected nothing. But he danced the only way a young man should: as if he wanted to woo me.

The lights and the leaves made shadow-puppet patterns all around. As the female saxophonist began a long virile improvisation, I put my head against my husband's chest and listened.

Where had he hidden it? The thing that was killing him? Dancing and laughing and flirting with me so happily—well, he hid it where we all hide it; it must be some feature of human existence that we have learned the magic trick, which is to place the gleaming coin on the heartline of your hand, close it in a fist and—presto!—a moment later the fingers open on a barren palm; where has it gone? It's there all along; through the whole marriage, it's there. It's a child's trick; everyone learns it, and how sad that we never guess, and go and marry a girl or boy who shows us an empty palm, when of course it's there in the crease of the thumb, the thing they want no one to see: the heart's desire.

"You're wearing Rediviva," he whispered.

I said I was.

"You never wear it."

I said I didn't know why; I'd found the bottle and something nostalgic had crept up. I could hear his heart beating rapidly.

He turned and looked at the band, breathing uneasily. "I think I'm going to have to sit this one out, I don't know what's come over me."

He leaned against a tree, and then a new song started, as slow as could be, with the sound of a million strings (really just two, multiplied by moonlight), and couples wandered the dance floor, trying to work out who was going to brave a slow dance after all those fast numbers. "He's too damn short," I heard a young girl whisper beside us, a fragrant gardenia in her hair, "He'll lean right into my chest." Holland had me dance with the soldier who had brought the drinks, so I smiled good-naturedly and let the young man lead me away. He took me in a slow, stiff circle beneath the long-limbed sycamores; he was one of those dancers who hums along to the music, and he did this as the band began, in a broken rhythm, to improvise on "Good As You Been to Me."

The particular shadows of the trees and the vibration of the young man humming, which carried along his arms and, faintly, onto my own body, called up something that was gone the instant I felt it. I clawed after it in my mind, and fell out of step, and had to smile and regroup myself, and tried to fall back into the rhythm, all the while focusing on this memory. It must have been a memory, but it was lost. We made another half circuit of the dance floor. Then he began to hum again, my partner, and it happened again—a kind of dazed sunlight fell over things—and this time I wouldn't let go of it: a rip in a shade, a tree shadow, a humming young man . . . then gone again, this time forever. Just a little piece of my youth that my brain had stored and, randomly summoned by this young soldier, had broken open as if in an emergency. Fading, but still faintly detectable: young Holland, hidden in his room, humming in my ear as he lay beside me on the bed. I looked at my partner, who couldn't have felt anything. I looked toward Holland, who was staring at me intently.

Something had been tugging at me throughout the dance, and it turned out to be just myself, as a girl, with some piece of the past to show me. And I could see that something was happening to Holland, too. Could it be that he saw, in the same flitting shadows of the leaves and the lights, the same orchestra playing slightly behind the beat, simply by random chance, a faint tracing of the past? Maybe just a crinkling of paper (a girl behind him finishing a candy bar) became Buzz turning the pages of a newspaper, years ago. Everyday, just as my snip of memory was everyday. Who was I to guess my husband's heart? I only know he looked so free from pain. We would be happy, each of us; this path I had taken, it was the right one. Life would continue on its proper course, filling the banks like a river undammed. No more doubt anymore. We kept each other's stare a long time, for we had each done a startling thing, dodged time for an instant—which is the only definition of happiness I know.

The music stopped. The singer in his silver tie said: "Ladies and gentlemen, it's time!"

My husband appeared beside me with more drinks, and from behind the bandstand, carefully monitored by Larkspur firemen, great jets of roaring sparks rose thirty feet into the air and we cheered, of course we yelled ourselves hoarse, why wouldn't we? That shimmering curtain descending; that firefall; the hiss and the sparks and their power to transport us; of course it scattered all cares, and of course he kissed me, as a sort of grateful goodbye, there on the dance floor, my old husband, my old love.

Holland left early, feeling unwell, and those drinks must have gone to my head, because I agreed to stay at the dance if he would arrange for my ride home later. He kissed me goodbye, saying he'd be fine and I should enjoy myself. Men kept asking me to dance, which I did, but mostly I kept with my humming soldier, perhaps with the magic thought that he'd bring back other shards of memory as well; he didn't. Instead, he performed the same fox-trot to every song, fancied up for fast numbers, softened for slow ones. Mostly what interested me was to be in a relaxed crowd, moving counterclockwise like skaters. For so long I had denied myself the feeling of being at home.

The young man—his name was Shorty—had been entrusted to take me back, and a cab waited for us outside, glowing like a telephone booth. Within, the driver peered intently at a book until Shorty rapped on the window and we were off.

"I saw how your husband kissed your hands when he said goodbye," he said. Silver branches of an apple orchard blocked the moon, and as we passed, I looked over to see his face emerging from the darkness. He had very large eyes, a mustache, and wire-rim glasses that gleamed like an etching.

"Oh, he's always done that. Since we were kids."

"You known him that long?"

"Well, long enough. I met him when I was sixteen, back in Kentucky."

"I'm from Alabama," he said. "He must be a real kind man."

"Yes, he is."

"You're lucky," he said, and added: "You know he's real good-looking."

"Oh," I said, looking out the window again. "Yes, he is good-looking."

In his voice, I seemed to hear a barely concealed desire: "He sure is."

So he was "one of them" as well. They were everywhere, these kinds of men, and I would forever be drawn to them. I sat back in my seat with a shudder, thinking of the changeling boys now being born, and the poor girls who someday would love them.

"You must love him a whole lot," he said softly.

He sat very silently, staring at me.

And I looked out the window, watching the moonlight hexing the mounds of the hills, the antlers of the trees, the shipless shore of the bay. The moon was rising quickly and had found a flock of clouds hidden in the sky and touched them all into vertebrated' streaks of light. Everywhere the stars struggled to show themselves. And farmhouses passed, sheds, windmills, all shining from the moon like china things.

Off in the distance a creature, perhaps a coyote, made a break for it across a hill, streaking like a comet in the moonlight.

"Missus Cook?" It was the young man again.

"Sorry, yes of course. He's a fine man."

"A beautiful woman like you deserves one."

We hit another stone and my hand fell between us, brushing Shorty's. I don't know why I didn't move it.

The driver struck a match and we were briefly bathed in that warm light before he touched it, gently, to his cigarette and then, when that was lit, thermometer-shook the match to darkness, leaving only a smoky question mark. I stared out at a house as it went past, then turned to look at Shorty and he kissed me.

That memory is as fresh as yesterday: the sensation of his arm around me and his hand moving down my collarbone to touch my breast in its corseletted cup; the smell of hair tonic in his curls as he leaned down to breathe erratically, somewhat desperately, saying: "You're so beautiful, you're so beautiful, Pearlie, I just want to . . ." Everything about the moment was young—the awkward frenzy of it, the gibberish he was talking, my own heart thrumming like a mad cricket, the rush and excitement of it all— but I don't think of us as young. In my memory, for those ten or twenty minutes, up to the moment I collapsed in laughter against the door and broke the spell, we were simply alive.

"Why are you laughing?" he asked, trying to smile himself while coaxing me back with his hands.

"Oh!" I said, but I couldn't explain. Here was the future I planned for myself. The moon and stars, the friction of another body, a match in the night. Here it was; it had not yet occurred to me, as it never occurs to any accomplice what will become of them once the crime is finished; they are too attuned to their role, their duties. Here was my life alone. And the thought was so astonishing, so pleasant and free, that I started to laugh like a child and couldn't stop, all the way back across the bridge. Shorty would take my hand and smile at me and try to kiss me, and once again I would convulse in laughter. Imagine that, with one of the most beautiful views in the world going by—that gemmy night-time view of the city with great golden pillars of the bridge looming on either side and the magnificent fog billowing and glowing beneath—and all I could do was laugh. I had got everything wrong; he wasn't "one of them" at all. He was a drunken young man grabbing a little joy while there was a moon and a paid driver and a woman he found beautiful. I could not guess what any man wanted; it was a tangle. And I forgave myself for laughing. There would be plenty of time when all of this was over, when I could breathe, and the inflamed, hopeful expression on Shorty's face is an image I will never forget.

He let me out at my home and I had hardly stepped out of the car before he put his hand on my arm. I was desperate for no one to see me out here with a young man. I leaned in and listened.

"Pearlie, couldn't you come back with me a minute?"

"No, no, I don't think so."

"Looks like your man's asleep. Just a minute, so we can talk. Not overnight."

It had never occurred to me to be with a man overnight.

"You gotta go," I said, shaking my head. "You can't just sit here."

He leaned back in the car and looked at me. Then, as he held out his hand, I found myself stepping back.

"Good night, Shorty," I said, signaling to the driver and spinning away. I swore I would not turn around; I swore I would not test the evening any further, but the thrill overtook me and I turned, briefly catching, from the speeding cab's rear window, those glasses gleaming back at me. Then he was gone.

The streetlamps cast elongated orbs of light through the fog. Only one house, its usually mown lawn neglected, had its lights on. The night had become warmer in the last few hours, like someone who has changed his mind a minute too late.

Strange to enter the house and hear nobody. And, though I knew that Holland would be in his bed, I felt as if I were actually alone, without even the soft purr of radio static or the white blank noise of an open window. I walked through the hall and into the living room, undoing the top button of my cardigan and looking around at the still darkness, the lonely expectant objects in their darkness: the yarn cat, the broken mantel clock. Me and my son, this is what it would be like.

A man was standing in the room with his back to me.

Drink made my heart beat happily. I said his name and he turned.

"Pearlie," he said.

"You're back! You want something to drink? What are you do-ing in the dark?"

He ignored my questions, looking at me intently. "Got back early. Finished everything. And Holland called me."

"Oh I see."

Buzz lowered his head. "He said he needed to say something to me, and when I got here—"

I said, "We went out dancing, he said he was sick—" I thought of Holland's dreaming stare that evening, the look of memory. "Well, good. That's what you wanted, isn't it?"

"Pearlie."

I laughed; I was still throbbing with drink and the touch of Shorty's lips on mine. "I think I don't mind anymore." I consid-ered Buzz in the glow of the window, pale as bone and as beautiful as I suppose he'd ever be. I said, "I've never seen you in moon-light. You'd make a handsome ghost."

"Pearlie, something terrible has—"

"I said I don't mind," I repeated, smiling.

"There was an accident. With a gun."

"What do you mean? What gun?" He said it again. I told him I needed to sit down, and yet I just stood there. "Is he all right?"

"Pearlie, I'll get you a drink."

I said I didn't want a drink; I wanted to know what he was talk-ing about.

In the war, a truck full of men used to drive around the Sunset with a bucket of brown paint and a ladder. They would climb up each streetlight and paint a dark hemisphere on the western half of the lamps so we couldn't be spotted by Japanese planes. From the east, a blazing city; from the west, an outline dark as the ocean. And that is what I did that night with Buzz. I darkened half my heart so what he said couldn't find me. I asked blankly: "Is he dead?"

He came toward me, saying, "They didn't tell anybody until the government men left, but once people saw them coming up the drive—"

"Government men?"

Buzz drank some of the brandy he had poured, and then said, "It was a drill, just a regular drill, and I guess something was wrong with his rifle—"

I looked at him now: "Buzz . . . what the hell are you talking about? Tell me what's happened to Holland?"

I have never seen a man look at me with such pity. It was a horrible expression. Every part of his face bent down with gravity and he put his hand on my arm. From the window, the glow of headlights came into the room and left again as if it had not found what it was looking for.

"Pearlie, it's not Holland," he said very firmly, his face white and grim, his gold hair shining in the light. "It's William. In boot camp. William Platt, a gun went off in his hand yesterday morning—"

"William Platt?" I said loudly.

"Yes, in a training exercise, running uphill—"

"I thought . . . you said 'he' and I . . . *William Platt* . . ." and then I mumbled something before I burst into tears.

Buzz came up to me in the doorway, his hands out to comfort me, but I turned away, shaking and gasping, weeping helplessly, leaning against the windowsill. He was talking to me, but I didn't hear anything else. I could only feel the warmth as he took me in his arms and held me, whispering things I do not recall. In my mind, William Platt marched gun-first up that Virginia hill into a great white mist, a quiet contentment beçalming his face, young William Platt who once called me a nigger, and despite everything, when Buzz had said that poor boy's name, all I could think of was my husband.

For I am a wife. And what I'd mumbled was: *"Thank God."*

IV

*A*merica, you give a lovely death.

That same summer, Ethel Rosenberg was electrocuted. The last time she saw her husband was minutes before he was taken to the chair, in a room where a screen separated the traitors so they could not touch. They were left alone; no one knows what they said to each other. But when the warden entered the room and separated the couple, leading Julius away, it is said he found the screen blotted with blood. They had tried to reach each other through the mesh; in a moment we can only imagine, they had pressed their fingers together with such passion that blood flowed down their hands.

"Be comforted then," she wrote her sons that day, "that we were serene and understood with the deepest kind of understanding, that civilization had not as yet progressed to the point where life did not have to be lost for the sake of life." Julius died instantly in the electric chair, and when they cleared his body away and led Ethel in, she was so small that the electrodes couldn't properly fit her head. When I read that it took two electric shocks to kill her, I sat down at my kitchen table and cried.

Why, Ethel, didn't you confess after Julius died? He was gone; there was no good to be done. I'll never know why you didn't pull the matron close to you and say anything to save your life, save your sons. Say anything they wanted to hear. You must know some secret I can't guess.

What is a wife? If they take away her children, her husband, her
house and belongings; if they send down a destroying angel to this
female Job and tear one son from her arms and another from the
schoolhouse so his textbook falls to the floor with a thud, send
agents to drag her husband from his home; if they take away the
telephone table in the hall; the geraniums wilting in the flower box
and the greens that have to be used before they go bad and the
new hat that she hasn't yet figured out how to wear? If they take
away the dog? If they take away her favorite wooden spoon? Her
brother? Her ring? What is the smallest atom of a wife that cannot
be split apart? Only you could ever say, Ethel, and you died silent.

Peace negotiations took place in a city in southern Korea, reestab-
lishing the old borders; no treaty was ever signed, but the war was
over. We did not win it, not in the way some wanted; we did not
chase the Communists back into China and unlock that country
for democracy, and men wrote to their local papers in disgust at
our cowardice. But we were sick to death of war, and we had held
the enemy back, so we left. Just one week after I heard about
William Platt. The harm we inflicted—it was all for nothing.

William Platt did not die.

Only in my imagination did he fall down in that Virginia mud
and never rise again. The loss of blood nearly took his life, but
luck was always with William. After twenty-four hours his young
heart beat regularly again; his eyes opened to the image of a lovely
nurse arranging flowers from his family. The doctors came and he
smiled, giving a thumbs-up with his remaining hand.

I watched my husband carefully. I might catch him listening to
the radio, his eyes wandering from one object in the room to the
next. I wondered what each sacrifice cost him. I wondered what
Buzz's arrival, Annabel's temptation, William's draft and injury
cost him, in the end, because even a man who reads a censored

paper sees the blanks and knows exactly how much has been cut to ease his mind. He must have known—the way a child knows—that all the strange events in his life were done for want of him, for possession of him. You couldn't see it, of course, as he leaned and listened to the radio, elbows on his knees. He seemed merely the handsomest man for a mile. But I knew the panic hung inside him, somewhere; a bat trapped in the rafters, folded and quiet all day while the rest of us were stirring, but night would come eventually. It would claw its way out; it had to.

William Platt's return was a neighborhood event, a hero's welcome. I watched from my window as the government car turned the corner and stopped before his mother's house, bedecked in patriotic colors. She ran out, a short woman with bright red hair, arms spread, but before William accepted her embrace, he turned to salute the driver with his left hand. His right arm ended, above the elbow, in a cocoon of gauze. Later, from infection, he would lose it all, and his young wife would lovingly alter his shirts, sewing the cuff of each right sleeve to his shoulder so it dangled like a flag. That day, Annabel ran to him, her blond hair curled in the rain. I remember how they embraced despite the downpour, how he grinned eagerly and she stroked his short hair desperately and he held her against his chest. Soon my window was speckled with rain, flattening the scene like a newspaper photo made up of dots. He was alive; he was a hero. I closed the drapes. It meant nothing; I had already taken on the guilt of a murderess.

There was a woman my grandmother knew, who owned nothing in the world but some pearls her great-aunt left her, and it was all she'd brought to her marriage: a strand of huge, luminous, beautiful pearls. Quite a treasure for a poor woman. One day there was a fire. The whole house burned down, and her sleeping husband burned with it. The woman came back from the trip she'd been taking, widowed, devastated to see the destruction and, picking through the wreckage, she discovered her scorched metal jewelry box. She opened it—and there were her pearls, as perfect, as beautiful as before only now absolutely black. The heat had done it. The friend who was with her wept: "They're ruined!" "Oh yes," said the woman, bringing them out, "they're ruined." But that was how she wore them, those blackened pearls; as a token, a holy relic around her neck.

The day William Platt stepped from that car, saluting with his one good arm, his wife sobbing beside him. The memory of that day. I wear it like that string of pearls.

People said that when America won the war, the burned-out marquee of the Parkside Theater relighted miraculously and glowed for a week. That was where I met Buzz at an ill-attended, midday double feature. It was one of our final meetings. We sat in the last row; a flash of sunlight brightened the movie screen above us. It was a war film. Prisoners stood in the cold white square of a yard, a warden addressing them in a language they did not know.

"What did we do?" Buzz whispered.

"It wasn't us. It wasn't our letter—"

"How do you know that?"

"There wasn't enough time," I said. "Things couldn't work so fast—"

"I suppose so."

"It's crazy to think they would take that letter seriously, change their draft rolls. You know the army. It wasn't us. It was chance."

A popcorn-box airplane came floating overhead—from kids in the balcony who paid their entrance fee with 7UP caps. A few rows before us, a man I knew to be deaf and dumb watched with sad fascination the pictures that were still silent movies to him.

A winter prison camp that had no walls, no fence, no barbed wire, as the warden loudly explained. During the day it was heavily guarded, but at night there was just a square of bright light in the middle of nowhere, the prisoners pinned there like

moths, and what kept them from escaping was the night, which
built its own walls, because all they could see beyond the blinding
whiteness of their prison was an impenetrable blackness. "It is the
Black Forest beyond, but you will never see it!" the warden
yelled. Their night was too black; their eyes would not adjust before they froze. He shouted: "You are blind men now."

Buzz said it was his fault.

"It was chance," I said again.

"I talked you into all of this."

"No, you didn't."

"You hid a boy from war," he told me, speaking close to my
ear. "I . . . I stood up back then and wouldn't go. I wouldn't kill.
I sacrificed things not to go to war. And now a boy—"

I shivered in the cold theater. "He never went to war."

A pause, then a whisper: "He did."

"What are you saying? It wasn't war. It was an accident."

He said, "We used him, Pearlie. Not in their battle but in
our own."

I turned to Buzz and saw in his eyes something I had never expected to see. Not in a man whose missing finger testified to his
unwillingness to fight. A general, in his tent early in the morning,
hearing the death toll from the push he has just ordered could not
have looked as battle weary. So stricken and sorry. It was the only
fight either of us was willing to join. The woman who hid her
man, the objector who found him. We would not fight to kill in a
war or to set the world aright, not for a country who disowned us,
but together we had found our cause. A prize so small it could not
be worth this sacrifice. Simply: ourselves.

"I could go away," he said in a pained voice.

"What do you mean?"

He took off his coat, struggling in the seat, not looking at me
but staring up at the screen. "If you asked me to. We've done
something bloody and terrible and ruined a life. Two lives. I
could leave tonight."

"And where would that leave me?"

"You'd go on as before."

"But I'd know he wanted someone else—not me."

"Maybe you and I should leave," he said. "I've sold everything, it's all done, you and Sonny could come with me."

On-screen, two prisoners played a pensive game of chess. Spotlights lit the parade ground as bright as a movie set, and within the bunkhouse bare bulbs hung glowing from the ceiling. In a flutter of death, one bulb extinguished itself. The prisoners stared at it, as did the guard, who paused a moment before shouting that a light had gone out.

"That's foolish talk," I said. "You didn't come to take me and Sonny away somewhere."

"I would do it."

"You'd get one mile out of town and start to think of him. You want to make amends to me, but it won't let you love him less. I don't understand it, but I've seen it. What brought you here won't let you leave."

"Take Holland, too."

I sighed aloud at that thought, and tried to see his face more clearly in the flickering darkness. I said, "No, Buzz. I can't do that. Take what you came for and leave me and Sonny be. It's too late."

Boos erupted from the balcony; the wrong reel had been inserted and now a woman from another century, her long blond hair in braids, a basket on her arm, kneeled beside a lake and tossed grass at a young man. He pulled a strawberry from her basket and she laughed with the abandon of youth. Quite wildly, he took her in his arms and kissed her, while the children in the balcony raged and threw their popcorn in the air. She struggled in his embrace, succumbing—and then the girl and her lover were gone. Cheers from above. The screen was winter-white, trapping Buzz and me in its glare.

A prison made entirely of light. So bright, so white, you can not imagine crossing over into the frozen darkness that surrounds you. Nothing keeps you from it; there is no electric fence or wall around a life, a marriage. Nothing really stops you from saving yourself, your son. It is just light, but it stuns you. It whitens the edges of you like frost. Years pass. The only thing that could spring you from such a prison is an error; a spotlight sputters out, a bulb, and you have a glimpse of the world around you. For a moment, you have your bearings; you see things clearly: how life could be. You look into each other's eyes, you nod, and in a fit of madness you take off across the border.

If Buzz left us, he'd return to the same starvation he had known once, years ago, but what we bear once we may not bear again. The bachelor's apartment; the single-burner stove; the album of photographs under the bed; a harmless, lonely life—he could not live it again. It was what brought him to my door, to skew the world a little, because to do otherwise—to sit and take the life you are offered—can be unbearable. He wanted to please, wanted to live it, but he couldn't. He did not take the step forward. And so the world lashed back—or no, it didn't. It did nothing at all. It kept spinning, as beautiful as ever, and silently looked on. "They didn't need to," as he told me once, when I had asked if they had hurt the prisoners. "We did it on our own."

The movie came back on; in the bunkhouse a shivering prisoner began to build a fire. Buzz looked across at me, and the space between us seemed as wide as a church aisle. He could not ask for what he wanted, which was a promise to stay with him, for someone to stay; if not Holland, then me; if not me, then the madness of solitude again. And he would not go back there.

"It's too late," I said.

He looked at me for a long moment before he nodded. Gratitude and love was on his face. Then, in one of those strange miracles of the cinema, an officer on the screen began to mirror

Buzz's movements: standing up, taking his hat, and walking
through a door that, swinging just like the theater door, produced the painful dazzling surprise of a sunny day.

It was only much later, when I learned the rest of his story, that I
fully understood what he had offered with those four words: "I
could go away." The solitary life he might have returned to. His
story of pain, which he told me at last. I have said that pain reveals
things, and that is sometimes what it takes to break our solitude.
To open, briefly, that small window, that view out of ourselves:
the life of someone else.

In the final days of the experiment, Buzz told me, his dreams
ransacked his memories, turning them into nightmares. His brain
recast familiar scenes like the train ride to Minnesota but this time
he appeared as a cannibal, running through the cars. Even his
memories were not safe; the hunger got to them, as well. This was
not as bad as the blackouts experienced by other men who would
lose whole afternoons. They arrived at their rooms unable to explain their absences, terrified of what they might have done. They
were not acting; they had gone mad. One spent days stealing fruit
from markets and erasing it from his memory. Another ate from
garbage cans; another stared at restaurant patrons for hours. And
one had to be sent away from the program for good. That was
Buzz.

It was the spring of 1945; peace was coming, though the boys
in Minnesota could never have known it. "We had almost forgotten about the war," he told me. "They told us it was nearly over,
and we would help the survivors, but it was very hard to think
about that." Six months had passed, and the starvation segment of
the experiment, at least, had come to an end. Hair was falling out;
lips and nails were blue; their flesh was puckered and gray, like the
skin of butchered animals. But they had survived it. "The stick

men," they called themselves, and would have laughed if they could. "The zombie soldiers." Buzz's mind began to glow again, faintly, at the notion that it was over. The hunger. A sturdy, dependable subject for all those months—an ideal subject, in many ways—no one could guess he was about to lose his mind.

It happened the day they announced the increase in food. Not everyone would get the same amount, the doctors said. The purpose of the experiment, they explained, wasn't, as the men had been led to believe, to find the best way to bring someone back to life. It was to find the cheapest way. Millions of hungry refugees wandered out of the cities of Europe, and the money had to go as far as possible to save them. There were so many mouths. The group had to find what was enough, what was too little. And so some men were given large portions of food, some less, some still less, and some barely more than they'd eaten all along. It was a bullet to the brain when Buzz heard he was part of this last group.

Apparently you cannot feed a starving man and expect gratitude. That is what they learned from the study, and later from the concentration camps. A man, nearly dead, will snarl at his plate of food. In that way, we are untamable.

He shouted several times a day at mealtime, taunting the men whose plates were two or three times the size of his; sometimes he refused his food altogether, tossing it onto the floor in a rage he could never explain. But he was a good subject; he pulled himself together. He told himself it would be over soon; this was not real life. It was just war; it was the life eventually you leave behind. It took all he had to sit at the table and eat the food they gave him, at least to stay alive.

"I don't remember," he told me, "what eventually happened to me." He accepted the refeeding system for about two weeks, and the doctors were surprised to see he began to lose instead of gain weight, because even his small diet was four hundred more calories than he'd eaten for half a year. Once again, he became irritable with doctors and with his fellow patients. He spoke to no one, read no books, would not even listen to the radio with his former friends. He would pour water into his plate and mush it like a milk shake, staring at the others as if daring them to do something about it. Eventually, though, he ate it with a spoon. He did not remember doing anything more unspeakable than this.

"They tell me I disappeared one afternoon, didn't show up for my physical, didn't leave any sign that I'd gone to town or anything. I suppose I blacked it all out, like the others. I don't remember. I can't explain it."

He did not remember being discovered in a garage. Or how a gleaming ax lay near him on the ground, among all the bits of metal, or how he crouched beside the workbench, involved in some activity. It was only when they got closer, he told me, that they noticed the blood freely flowing from his left hand and watched, with horror, as—delicately, lovingly—he fed himself tiny gobbets of his flesh.

This is a war story. It was not meant to be. It started as a love story, the story of a marriage, but the war has stuck to it everywhere like shattered glass. Not an ordinary story of men in battle but of those who did not go to war. The cowards and shirkers; those who let an error keep them from their duty, those who saw it and hid, those who stood up and refused it; even those too young to know that one day they would rise and flee their own country, like my son would, when his time came to go to war. The story of those men, and of a woman in a window, unable to do a thing but watch.

I saw it all. Holland Cook silhouetted in his hiding chamber and years later on a gray beach, staring at the sea that had swallowed him. William Platt home from Virginia in his uniform, wife running to him, smiling as he saluted with his one remaining hand.

Buzz Drumer rubbing his hand as his "tell" in conversation, and blasted with grief in the white light of that movie theater, greeting the return of his own madness. Sonny's voice on the phone, the day I would get his draft card, years later. I saw it and thought, "I'll save this one." A reprieve for one man, a release from the turning wheel. Surely the world won't miss one more. Surely there has been enough.

It is madness not to do as you are told. Not to step forward from a hiding place, a deferral, from a line of frightened young men. But it is astounding how different men are; not all from the same clay, for when it comes to the kiln, some break wide open or change in ways even the maker can't predict.

Where is the dollar bill for those men? For the cowards, the shirkers? Like the one Buzz gave me, by accident, on our first meeting by the sea? Covered with the signatures of nineteen-year-old soldiers headed off to war. Sitting in bars and signing dozens of bills, using them to pay for drinks, hoping their memory would still circulate after they shipped off, and fought, and died for their country.

There is nothing like that for the boys who did not go to war; they were not soldiers, and did not die. They are burned out of history, for nothing blazes quite as hot as shame. There are no bills in circulation. But I have signed their names to this story. I have signed all of our names.

How else will we be remembered?

A few nights later, a succession of streetcars took me far from the Sunset. I was no longer Pearlie Cook; I was a stranger in a cloth coat and cat-whisker bow, a mystery on the tramline, a colored girl clutching her purse, headed who knows where. This was not unusual for most people, used to being surrounded by strangers, nothing expected of them. At one point, the streetcar lost its electricity and the driver had to walk outside with a long pole to reconnect the wires, and as we sat in darkness, the man across from me gave me three glances: my legs, my hands, my eyes. I could be any girl, headed anywhere. A late-night shift at a factory, a date at a nightclub, an affair out at the farthest edge of town. The car awakened with light and he gave me one more appraising look before he got off at his stop. No one ever glanced at Pearlie Cook, but I was someone else that night.

As a WAVE, I had always considered taking a streetcar to its very last stop, and now that I lived at the very end—nothing is more final than an ocean—I traveled backward to downtown, and in a quiet, dreamlike state, I made my way to where Chinatown met North Beach, to the spot where sailors have been coming since the Gold Rush. It used to be called the Barbary Coast. It wasn't called that in my day. It was called the International Settlement—it said that, in fact, spelled out in huge metal letters over the archway on Broadway.

The priests had long ago doused the red lights, so it was probably only half as seedy as a hundred years earlier. Coffee shops and bars full of long-haired poets, bearded radicals. One particularly elegant woman, in a melon-sleeved princess coat and a daisy veil, could have been transported that instant from Paris. All that gave her away was her walk (horribly burlesque) and her eyes, fishing everywhere for a customer. She even caught my glance and gave me a pleasant snarl. I didn't mind; I had been given worse in soda shops. She passed under the blade sign of a dance hall (MADAME DUPONT: DANCES FIFTY CENTS) and was lost in its atomic neon glow.

There it was, at the corner of Broadway and Kearny: a bar called the Black Cat. It had been there since the thirties. No windows, barely a sign, but it seemed full when the door swung open and revealed a bare bulb hanging, black or nearly black walls, posters tacked to them, a man standing just inside the door with a basket of buttons. I stood there for an hour as he handed them to transvestites with a smile, and the "ladies" would pin them to their.

stuffed bosoms or their hats, laughing, and walk inside. I later got close enough to read one, and found it said: I AM A MAN. The bar had been turned inside out by police every week or so, on the pretense of a law banning deliberate intent to pass for the opposite sex. So to keep from being arrested they wore these buttons. I heard later that the men inside—not just the transvestites but all of the men—stood a few feet apart from one another, because there was a law about that, too.

I didn't go inside. I just stood and watched the men. Two fairly young ones came out, laughing, smoking cigarettes, coat collars turned up against the night air, white shirts and black ties like clerks. Lovers, I assumed. It amazed and terrified me to see people name their desires so freely, so easily, as if there were nothing to lose; as if it were as simple as pinning them on like a button. The men stubbed their cigarettes out against their shoes in a kind of dance, and then field-stripped them—tore them apart so the tobacco floated in the air. A soldier's habit. So the enemy couldn't track them.

An older man in a cowboy hat arrived and put his hand on the shorter man's shoulder. They spoke for a moment before going inside together, and the men I had been watching exchanged a single smile before only one was left, looking defiantly around. Not lovers, then. I could not get anything right.

But I did sense something. Beyond the inscrutable movements of these men, the world they had built beneath the ordinary one; beyond the seedy lights and grimy hotels, the hauntings of sex that had not changed for a century; it was a feeling, which I could not name at the time, of something awakening. It was happening all around me, in the bookstore across the street, in the cafés, and in the bars. It was as if part of the body was stirring, moving very slowly to rouse the rest. Some change was coming; I was part of it. The way we lived would not do, would not hold. A decade from now, and nothing would be familiar in this spot. Not even me.

I won't pretend I saw it clearly then. That, looking at the man outside, at the Black Cat, I didn't grapple with disgust or outrage or that most unforgivable of self-deceits: pity. Certainly I pitied that young blond man. Even as I was willing to grant Buzz what he wanted, what I assumed my husband wanted, even as I saw it more and more as a real kind of love, I pitied that man on the street.

Seen from a distance, the scene is comic. After the sailor passed, the young man caught my gaze. We regarded each other for a moment and he smiled at the colored girl in her old hat. As our eyes met across that dark street, I understood. That I pitied him no more than he pitied me.

I went home on the streetcar oddly warmed by what I had seen, determined to see out the course of the next week, the last one of my former life. I was like a thief in his hideout, drinking cold coffee, reading every day in the paper about the baffled cops, with only one week left to wait, one week before it's safe, and he can sneak back to where he hid the diamonds.

I have a rendezvous with life . . .

"Market and Duboce!" the conductor shouted. "Sunset Tunnel ahead!"

The wedding of the younger aunt took place at a colored church in Santa Rosa, cactuses blooming in pots by the door, the bride dressed all in blue. Sonny carried the ring, and of course dropped it, giggling, at the proper moment. Alice giggled as well. I have rarely seen a look of such satisfaction on a woman's face, but even greater was that of the groom: elegant, portly, and handsome, he kept smiling, looking up at the one pane of stained glass—our Lord Jesus Christ ascendant—as one would look at a man who had lost a friendly wager. The eldest sister stood beside her, holding the small bouquet of yellow roses, listening carefully to the preacher, nodding at every period in his sermon. He spoke of God's time and our time. I saw that Holland wept a little when his old aunt kissed her groom. The only audience was a few old women with fans and loud "Amens," and when it was over and the couple was being congratulated, I left with Sonny to find a restroom. When I let him run back inside, and was alone in the hallway, I noticed a middle-aged woman hiding behind the door, looking inside. She wore a small yellow hat, a flower pinned to her dress, and an expression of grim determination.

"Which one is the bride?" she asked in a small, sharp voice. She must have come at the very end of the ceremony.

I introduced myself, and she said hello before announcing solemnly: "I'm his daughter. From his first family."

"I didn't know he had another family."

"Oh yes," she said. "Oh yes."

I said it was a shame she'd never met my aunt before, but she shook her head. "Oh he never did dare show her to us. He carried on with her when I was just a little girl. Still married to my mother, oh yes. Now she's dead and here they are. I didn't come to see the wedding, I'm not a masochist. I just wanted to get a good look at her."

She peered discreetly into the room, searching the faces. The aunt: a mistress. And here, slipping the preacher a twenty: the married man whose loss had left its own mark on young Alice. He must have considered leaving his family for her, throwing it all over long ago, but at last came to his senses and returned to his family. Perhaps the eldest sister had a hand in it. Only now, when everything was over, and they were old, and sensibilities no longer mattered, had he returned. And Alice had accepted him. I had not bothered to look at the whole of that woman's life, her hidden reserves of rebellion.

"Do you have brothers or sisters?" I asked.

"Oh yes, but we weren't invited. He knows how we feel. Tell me which one she is. I want to see her face."

I pointed out Alice in the corner, talking to the preacher.

The woman shook her head adamantly. "That ain't her."

I said it certainly was.

She smiled. "I heard how beautiful she was. It was just like him, to be tempted by a beautiful woman. My mother was all that kept him in line. He couldn't turn away from a pretty face. Which one?"

I stood in wonder at her words. I had seen pictures of the aunts. They were solid, intelligent women, wonderfully dressed. But they had never been beautiful.

"I tell you that's her."

She stared at the scene intently as her father made his way across the room, took his new bride's hand, and kissed her on the lips. The preacher quietly applauded.

"Can't be," she said, then tore the flower off her dress, threw it on the ground, and walked away without another word.

I stood in the doorway and watched her get into her car and angrily speed off. Alice and her groom emerged, and Sonny, who had been entrusted with the rice and could hardly stand the suspense, began tossing it wildly into the air. None of it touched the married couple—nothing could touch them—as they made their careful way, holding hands, down the stairs and toward the small reception we had planned. The eldest aunt was approaching; I was meant to help with the food. I took a deep breath, glad that no one had witnessed the scene with the daughter. I suppose it had been unforgivable for that old man, in his wild youth, to have considered breaking everything for a plain girl. An ordinary girl, shy and doubtful of her charms. The tragedy of her family, averted, only to reappear. The daughter must have realized, seeing that old woman dressed in blue, that it had not only been the heat of passion that had flared in her father decades ago. The temptation of mere beauty. She would have accepted that as how men were, no threat to her mother's memory. But here was something senseless, enraging, beyond understanding. At least for a stranger to love.

"Sonny, that's enough rice now. Pearlie, are you coming? I need you to bring out the egg salad, I've got my hands full with—"

"Of course, Beatrice, right away."

The next day, I made my last atonement.

It was a small house, one of the older models, without the additions of a turret or a sunken living room, and from the outside there was something a little shabby about it beside its more glamorous neighbors; no one had yet cleaned the sea grime off the stucco or repainted the trim. But, through an open picture window, you could see the inside was different. The walls were freshly painted in inexpensive "milk paint": blue pastel in the visible parlor. A junkyard spinning wheel sat as homely as an old maid in the corner, webbed with satin thread. The cheaply, ingeniously furnished house of newlyweds.

No one seemed to be home; I walked up with my envelope, careful that nobody should see me. Below an old-fashioned twist doorbell sat the blank open mouth of a mail slot. In it went; done. I stepped behind a juniper. And I assume it was the faint sound of that envelope hitting the floor that brought her suddenly to the picture window.

I was just a foot away from Annabel. One hand sat on her hip, holding a feather duster, her hair up in a kerchief; she looked around, but I was well hidden and had the luxury of watching her from the shadows. A second glance told everything. For Annabel Platt was pregnant. The brown fabric of her apron made no excuses for it, and in a moment she had shifted into the classic pose of motherhood: the saintly hand on the belly, the chin receding slightly into the fat of the neck.

She saw the envelope, then disappeared for a moment, returning with it in her hands. I saw her look around again, but I was in shadow. Then, as Annabel Platt opened it with her long white fingers, her face hardened into astonishment. One by one, she counted out five thousand dollars.

There is no final forgiveness for the things we do. The awful part is that it goes on forever. What happened to William Platt, and to young Holland Cook. I felt, rightly or wrongly, that it happened because of me. They killed Ethel because she would not "deter" her husband; but my crime was far worse. I was willing to step in and alter a war, and a marriage, and the course of several lives. That is how I see it. It may be a childish torment, but we do not get to choose our demons.

Annabel's hand went once again to her belly. A faint smile. Then, as I watched her put those bills back into the envelope and place it on a side table webbed with lace, I knew it was over. I had atoned—or had begun my atonement—for the shipwreck I had made of things. Perhaps imagining the changes she could now make in her life—the classes she could return to, the help for William, for her baby—she touched the spinning wheel and set it in motion, and we both watched, together, as it turned on its wobbling axis.

That particular day had a noisy, foreign beauty to it. Italian churches and cement temples white and pink beside the ocean, fragrant eucalyptus, spiny century plants and yucca, all lit from the west by a bright clear sun. Outside my house, the sky was a fat lovely blue, streaked with airplanes, with a sun everywhere at once, stirring things into action—people were out as if on a holiday, raucous as a crowd of birds.

As I came to the open door, I could see Holland in the hallway, staring out of a window, his hands in the pockets of his suit, wearing an expression of peace. Bright and unfocused, looking up beyond the roofs of the houses, his shoulders low and relaxed against the wall, his sleeves rumpled from where his hands sat loosely in his pockets, his watch catching the light and flashing like a heliograph; a mind ajar. Unbolted like the window he looked through, his thoughts blowing gently. It was like seeing a map unfolded on a table, the creases pressed flat so it lay spread out wide; a map to places I had been with him, and if I stood there long enough I might see at last how they all connected.

What do you want from life? Could you even say? I know I could not, even when Buzz Drumer came and asked me. But part of us must know, and I think that's what I saw on Holland's face, that day in the hallway. It was as if he had been turned inside out, and all the secret wants, the longings of his youth, showed everywhere on his skin, like the bright hidden lining of a glove. When for a moment he saw what he wanted.

The very next moment, Holland noticed me, smiled, and was about to speak when a small voice came from the other room: "Lyle's back!"

My son and my dog were both upon me, each more desperately happy than the other. Lyle pawed at my dress, and I leaned down to hold him; he licked my face and shivered in a frenzy of love.

"It's a miracle!" Holland said, grinning down at us. "We were out on the lawn, and Sonny started shouting. We saw him coming down the street."

"I can't believe it!" I said.

"Poor Lyle, he was running as fast as he could."

Sonny said, "Lyle peed everywhere!" and then the dog leaped away, full of an energy I had not remembered. Sonny seemed to think he was chasing his mute friend, but Lyle in his turn seemed intent on chasing Sonny. They scampered out into the kitchen, froze in tense positions of attack, and then, when Sonny yelled his name, both animals leaped at each other, then fell onto the hall rug between me and my husband, rolling with open mouths and lolling tongues before they fell to a panting stop. Someone once wrote about two old friends like these, wondering how long they could have stared into each other's eyes. Forever?

"When?" I asked.

"About two hours ago," my husband said, watching them. "Where were you?"

"Dropping off something. Where had he been?" I asked, and then laughed at myself for thinking anyone could ever know.

My husband smiled. "I guess he was done with adventures. It looks like he had one or two."

Was it just Lyle's return I'd seen on his face? A lost dog running down the street might be enough for anybody. Fur flying everywhere in the sun, tongue hanging from his mouth, eyes bright in recognition of the family he loved, of the familiar smells sparking in his brain, and of his own great luck. Perhaps it was enough to leave my husband's face as open as I'd seen it in the hallway. Or was there more? I believe that while I was in North Beach, Buzz had visited the house and taken his old lover on a long walk by the ocean. Perhaps at last he said, *Come back to me*, as I had done years before on the streetcar tracks. He had spoken the right words. Ones that urge our hearts to action, always the same: *Let me take care of you.*

Later, Buzz told me that the date was nearly set, that he would be leaving early one morning and Holland would come with him: "Pearlie, you have to get ready for the thought that soon you'll be alone." Not until he said that did I truly picture what we had been planning: as plain as Holland getting in a car. All the anguish and plotting came down to the slam of that door. But what I also understood, for the first time, was that I would be losing Buzz as well. It had all seemed an impossible fantasy, and now I heard

Buzz saying: "I've told him what I want, how I never could forget him in all those years." It was that show of passion that always moved my husband, had taken him from Buzz's life into my own, and now would return him to his habitat. The passion of others. "He's like a mirror that way," Buzz told me. It was the truest thing he ever said about Holland Cook.

On the day of his return, gnawing gingerly at my son's hand, Lyle lay on the floor, skinny and matted with burrs. Everything golden about him was tarnished, dirty; I assumed it never occurred to either male to give the dog a bath; he looked like a free animal, owned by nobody. Yet he had come home. Perhaps, like most of us, he was too domesticated in the end.

"You love us, don't you?" Holland asked, teasingly, rubbing the dog's belly, and Lyle closed his eyes in pure delight. "We forgive you, you crazy thing."

If Lyle could have howled to the skies, I'm sure he would have.

The last time I saw Buzz alone, it was in an unloved park. Young poplars filtered the light, and nettles crowded the shadows where, like frightened birds beaten from the underbrush, a pair of lovers quickly emerged and hurried off to their parked car. We descended to the clearing, unkempt except around two stone plinths that marked the last duel in California. Hardly anybody visited the spot. I was the one who had found it on the map and suggested it; we had nearly run out of places to meet. We did not, however, need any more places.

"You have to tell me," I said.

He paused and looked at me seriously. "Tomorrow."

"You leave tomorrow? That's too soon, you didn't say—"

"It's tomorrow, Pearlie," he said. "That's what you and I talked about, and it's the best thing. I don't want to delay; it's all so delicate with him. The Chinese say to be happy, you must be swift." I wondered if the Chinese really said that.

I examined his face carefully. "You've told him?"

He ran his hand through the leaves of a bush. "We had a long talk the other night."

"You've told him everything." He nodded. "You've told him about me."

"Yes."

"What did you say?"

He pulled off a leaf and spread it in his hand. "That I would take care of you and your son."

"He knows I'm not abandoning him?"

"Nobody is abandoning anybody," he said, looking up. "He knows. That you understand and this is what you want for Sonny."

Birds were fussing in the trees. "That's not quite how I would have said it."

"Then I apologize. I did the best I could. I've been so anxious." .

I turned to him and asked, at last: "Doesn't he love you?"

Buzz turned the leaf in his hands and stroked the small ridge of veins, smiling. He said, "He does. I know it for sure now."

I thought of what I had seen the other day, in the hallway of our house: a man with his mind ajar. A face at last legible, a truce with something inside himself. "Yes," I said for certain. "Somehow I needed to know that."

He walked along in silence for a moment, taking the leaf apart bit by bit. "Thank you," he said.

"What for?"

"You were kind to me."

I leaned against the stone plinth, marked with the name of a duelist. "We are friends, you know," I said. "Despite everything."

"It doesn't seem likely," he said. "But I'm glad to hear you say it. Despite everything."

The sound of a truck came rumbling by, somewhere beyond

the trees, and a boy began shouting in a foreign language. I asked if he had mentioned Annabel and he shook his head.

"So he doesn't know everything," I said.

"Does he need to?" he asked, and I didn't reply. We had done enough.

"So tomorrow."

He threw the leaf into the grass as he walked along. "That's right. I thought maybe Holland could put Sonny to bed."

"But I'm the one who does that, it'll seem—"

He stopped and looked at me. "That'll be his time," he said. "Holland's time, you know . . . to say goodbye."

A brief dread shot through me as I imagined Buzz and Holland coaxing a sleepy Sonny out of his bed, fists rubbing eyes, into a waiting car . . . but it was quickly replaced with my husband standing in my son's dark room, nodding his head and turning away. He was a loving and attentive father. Buzz had promised his presence in my son's life, letters and visits and, later, trips with Sonny; the duties of a father, which Holland would never truly abandon.

"And what then?"

Buzz kept walking, going through the evening. "Maybe you and Holland listen to the radio the way you always do." That would be my time.

Buzz continued: "And then at ten he'll say it's time for bed—"

"After Groucho."

"After that," he said, pulling aside an overhanging branch. "He'll say it's time for bed and you'll kiss him good night or whatever you do, just whatever you normally do. You might take a sleeping pill."

I asked him why I'd need one of those.

"It might be easier on you."

"Easier on you," I said. "If I just sleep through it."

"I have some if you want to borrow them," he said, reaching into his pocket. He had planned it out so far as to bring a potion for me.

"No, I have some."

He looked intrigued—that I was still, at the last moment, so full of surprises—then walked on. "Then you and Lyle go to sleep and that's it," he said, caressing the old wound on his hand, squinting as the sun came through the leaves and flashed for a moment. "I'll leave you some money on the table. And then more later."

I watched as he crossed the grass before me. "You'll be there? Tomorrow night?" Somehow this hadn't occurred to me. "When?" I asked Buzz. "I want to know."

He said he would come at around eleven o'clock, by the back door. "We'll load his bags in the car and some other things. I hope you don't mind, we may take the radio and some of his favorite books."

It felt, all of a sudden, like the strangest thing that could ever happen to me. I said, "You're telling me I'll wake up and find things missing and be all alone with my son."

He saw my expression. "Pearlie . . . we've talked about all this—"

"I just hadn't realized—"

His face convulsed in sympathy and confusion. "Isn't this what you wanted?"

I laughed. Because he'd never asked either of us what we wanted. Not me or my husband, not really. He would have said he'd tried to, that he'd shown us vistas and options, the variety of possibilities, and we had stood mute before them. So he said what he wanted and asked if we'd go along. I don't blame him. You cannot sit around and wait for other people to figure themselves out. You would wait forever. Half of life is knowing what you want.

He said, "I don't understand . . ."

What I wanted, now that we had come to it, was so far from what he had shown me. More than the freedom of solitude, of five hundred acres with a fence all around. I wanted to have been born in a different time, in a different part of the world, so I could one day know the sensation that Buzz took for granted—that of naming your desire and feeling the right to possess it.

"Buzz Drumer," I said. "What's going to become of you?"

I remember his smile as I approached. I am not likely to forget that face, though I last saw it so long ago. I still see it, like a rubbing made from a church engraving, which believers can admire years after the church has burned down. He watched me quietly the entire time I came to him across the grass.

I put the bird of my gloved hand over his ruined one.

Buzz looked into my eyes and then he kissed me. It seemed like a very natural thing to do: kissing a boy before he leaves for war. A flicker of grief and desire. I never thought I'd miss him, on our last day. I was too busy preparing for a new life, a new world for my son. But I would miss the sound of that voice, the broken nose, the hat left on the seawall. Fainter and fainter as the years went on, until just those separate parts of him remained. A faded fresco in my mind. It's the loss we don't speak of, losing a friend forever. We call it life; we call it time passing. But it is a kind of heartbreak, like any other.

"What's going to become of you, Pearlie Cook?"

"Give us time," I said.

Buzz looked at his watch and said the words "ten o'clock." He gave a quick wave of his hand and walked away from me down the path. I watched his hat move through the leaves until it disappeared in the greenness of the grove. I waited for ten minutes or so before I started home. Tomorrow. Ten o'clock and I would take the pill. Eleven and he would come as I slept. By midnight, they would be gone.

I'm sure that day was no different from any other for Sonny. I awoke him whispering "Good morning, sweet boy" and Lyle came in to bother him until he stood up, grumbling; he drank his milk and ate his toast, cut with a measuring cup into a moon. We visited the park, which was mercifully free of other children. Back home, he took his nap with his odd hand puppets. He slept for twenty minutes while I stared at the clock, and after who knows what dreams, Sonny woke grumpier than before, so I spent a difficult hour coaxing him onto the sofa with a picture book. For the fortieth time I read aloud about a bunny that went inside a hill, and as Sonny gradually fell under its hypnosis, my mind began to wander. Two hours, now. Holland would be home in two hours, and then dinner, and then bedtime, and then the radio.

Suddenly, of all things, we watched through the picture window as a bird flew straight into the glass with a bang.

You'd never guess what grown-up Sonny remembers from his childhood. Not the aunts bustling around our house; not his best friend Lyle, who lived just two more years. Not Buzz Drumer. "I remember your stockings had gold diamonds on them with a *P*," he tells me when he comes to visit. "And you losing a ring behind the dresser. And I remember a bird flying into the window and how it scared me."

Who can fathom a boy's life?

A noise from the street—whirr, up and around went Lyle like a top! Sonny's father was home. His hat came off, a warm smile came on, and boy and dog raced to greet him. Sonny told him all about the bird at the window and his father listened patiently and accepted the whiskey I handed him. Noodles for dinner, eating while gabbing away at his father, Lyle waiting below for some dropped macaroni. Then a bath, more solemn than usual, asking, "Mommy, will I go down the drain?" He tried the white rubber duck; it did not fit. Then the cold shiver before the towel, and the naked race through the house—caught at last by his father. "Why don't you tuck him in tonight?" "Well . . . sure if you like."

His father tucked him into warm sheets, and read him the bunny story and the duck one again, and then, as Sonny struggled against sleep at this miracle of his father's presence, Holland began to speak in a low, serious voice.

❧

"He made me read two stories," Holland said as he came back in, settling himself into the big armchair.

"Well he knew he could get away with it," I said from the couch.

"What's on the docket tonight?" he asked, as he always did.

"News, then Groucho, then bed I think."

"After a drink, I hope."

"Naturally," I said.

It was eight o'clock. Holland touched the knob of the radio beside him and it came to life: *Morgan Beatty News*. For the first few moments, the fabric thrummed visibly against its wooden cage, as if Mr. Beatty sat inside, breathing against the burlap, and after it settled down I smothered an impulse to say, "You should fix that." Holland lit a cigarette and listened peacefully. Mr. Beatty went on about the hundredth suicide at the Golden Gate Bridge, Mrs. Dian E. Black, revealed now to be a phony. As I saw it, if I'd asked Holland to "fix that," he would have turned his solemn face to me and said there were three hours remaining of his life in this house. In which of them should he fix the radio? Instead, he sat in the sunset glow of the lamp, smoking his cigarette, listening to the fake note that Mrs. Black had left—"Sorry, but I had to go"— and staring at the masking-tape pot on the shelf. The time for all that was over. He picked a piece of tobacco from his lip.

"Another?" I asked, and he smiled.

"Oh, make it a double." The old chuckle. "One for you, too."

I brought up another glass.

"There you go," I said as I set his drink down and took a cig-arette. It was nearly nine.

He automatically held a flame up to my face. *Goodbye*, I thought as the cigarette lit with a hiss. He flicked the lighter closed and smiled.

"I saw Mrs. Platt the other day," I said. "William's mother."

He seemed a bit startled by this. "Did you?"

"Annabel's opening a shop on Maiden Lane."

"Downtown," he mused, sipping from his drink. "People can afford the wildest things."

"Her father must be helping her out. William's taking over when the baby comes."

He laughed, and I asked what was so funny. "Oh nothing," he said. "Men helping women out with their businesses."

"It's a new world," I said.

"It sure is."

At nine thirty, Groucho came on the radio. My husband sat still, staring, like the portrait of a war hero. Then, for a second, the radio cut out and I could hear the clatter of the ice in his drink. I looked and his hand was shaking. I caught his careful glance, and in those eyes: a look of dazzling pain.

The awful strain he must have been under, that night. I'm sure in his delicate, transposed heart—a heart that in its way existed—he felt at last the weight of what he had done. For in a way we had not done it; he had done it. By being what everyone wanted him to be—being the husband, the flirt, the beautiful object, and the lover—by pleasing us all in giving us his gracious smile, he had tortured each of us when it did not turn our way. Beauty is for-given everything except its absence from our lives, and the effort to return all loves at once must have broken him. As I saw it, he was choosing one love—the loudest love, the purest—and in choosing Buzz, he felt the others collapse around him. Mine, and Annabel's, and everyone's he met on the street. He could not have held them up forever. It was a childish notion to think he ever could, childishly cruel. And that was what I saw in his eyes; the look of a man forced, at last, to leave the possibilities of youth behind. To figure out the heart's desire. I saw, from the look of pain there, how truly sorry he was.

What is it like for men? Even now I can't tell you. To have to hold up the world and never show the strain. To pretend at every moment: pretend to be strong, and wise, and good, and faithful. But nobody is strong or wise or good or faithful, not really. It turns out everyone is faking it as best they can.

Groucho had ended, the applause drowned by a wave of static. Holland reached over to click off the radio.

"I guess it's time for bed," he whispered.

"I suppose so."

"I'm beat. I really am," he said, then turned to me: "Pearlie . . . ?"

"What's that?"

He held my gaze for a long time without saying anything—it was not in him to say those words—but I knew, from his expression, what he meant. It was what we had never discussed, what he probably had wanted to say the night of the air raid and had lost his chance; here was the last he would ever have: "Tell me now if this is what you want."

I was still in my twenties. And here's what I thought would be the worst: that no one else would ever know me young. I would always be this age or older, from now on, to any man I met. No one would ever sit back and remember how young and frail I was at his bedside, at eighteen, reading to him in that dark room with the piano playing downstairs, and again at twenty-one, how I held the flap of my coat against the wind and held my tongue when a handsome man called me by the wrong name. What I would miss—and it occurred to me only then, with his brown eyes on me—was the unchangeable, the irreplaceable. I would never meet another man who'd met my mother, who knew her untamable hair, her sharp Kentucky accent, cracked with fury. She was dead now, and no man could ever know her again. That would be missing. I'd never know anyone, anywhere, who'd watched me weeping with rage and lack of sleep in those first months after Sonny was born, or seen his first steps, or listened to him tell his nonsense stories. He was a boy now. No one could ever again know him as a baby. That would be missing, too. I wouldn't just be alone in the present; I would be alone in my past as well, in my memories. Because they were part of him, of Holland, of my husband. And in an hour that part of me would be cut off like a tail. From that night on, I would be like a traveler from a distant country that no one had ever been to, nor ever heard of, an immigrant from that vanished land: my youth.

No, Holland, not what I wanted. Too late, now, to ask, if that was now what you were doing. I could not tell. What I wanted was you, but not you as I had always known you. Not the boy in the room, anymore; not the soldier on the beach, misremembering my name. It was not enough to live on. Not once the flood had come, to wipe it all away; it was not enough to replace things just as they were. You as you were. I had lived like a woman whose lonely house, it was rumored, had a treasure buried in its walls. It was enough to dream of it, but once those walls had been torn down, the rooms strewn with plaster, I could not live there. Not that I could regret the chance I took—what else is life for?—but I would not be a dreamer, a keeper, a hiding place. The world was about to change, and I could feel it. And I was still young. I would change with it.

I gave no answer. Instead, I cleaned up the glasses, put away the bourbon. I walked to my bedroom and then, without meaning to, I turned and said, "Goodbye."

He stared as if he might have heard me wrong. I will never know what he thought I said, there in the doorway; I will never know because he is dead now, and I had only meant to say "Good night," but at that moment it seemed possible our lives had gone unsaid for a minute too long. It seemed possible we were going to say all the things we had left unspoken. That he would stand there and say "Tonight I'm going to run away for love" and I would fold my arms over my breasts and say "Tomorrow I'm going to try it alone" and we would stare at each other, chalked by the hall light, and it seemed possible we would strike each other, wail and beat each other for what we had done, what we had taken without asking—the silent breakfasts and grinning dinners, the countless hours of each other's lives—nothing more or less than a marriage.

But Holland did not speak. He reached for a pack of matches from his breast pocket, and then he looked at me with a curious expression. His eyes went large and his mouth collapsed at the edges, like something left in the rain, and despite everything I had the sudden urge to rush over and comfort him.

Had he heard me say it? I will never know. He just replied, softly, "Good night," then smiled at me and went into his room. The door clicked shut; I heard the mechanism of the lock. I went into my own room, scented with spilled perfume, and watched as Lyle lay down on his sheepskin. Every light in the house went out. And then all was quiet.

It was ten fifteen when I took the doctor's pill; it felled me like an ax.

When I was a girl, the Green River flooded our town. A line on the courthouse, engraved with the year 1935, marks where water rose above the heads of full-grown men. I remember how the tops of the apple trees broke the water all around us in green islands, their branches heavy with floating fruit. I remember how frightened my parents were. We waited as the water rushed by in the darkness. And I was young. I had no idea that it would ever end. I thought that maybe this was how we would live now.

That was the form my dream took, under the influence of that pill. I was back in that old house, with my parents, and the water rising up and lapping against the porch; the green apples drifting by like planets. But in my dream we stood there for some reason unsure of what to do. "Secure the windows!" I kept saying, and they looked at me very afraid, unmoving: old people. And the water kept rising higher, dark and viscous around our ankles. "What do we do?" they kept asking. "What do we do?" I knew it, someone told me once. How do you survive a flood? Do you leap in the water, on anything that will float? Each on his own box or table? Or do you huddle together in the attic? I could not remember. One was right, and one was terribly wrong. It was like a test, in school, on which everything hinges. And still the water was rising. "What do we do?" my mother begged. Then I remembered. I told her, and in that dream the moment I told her— her old face broadening in a rare smile—for some reason I heard myself saying, clear as anything, as if it were not even a dream: "How could I have gotten it so wrong?"

The next morning, I was awakened by a lion's roar—the nearby zoo. I lay there a long time in my bed. Oh Lord, I thought. The light shifted on the ceiling like pages turning in a book, blank, unwritten pages. I think I was still dazed from the pill. Yet everything was as calm and clear as glass and I knew, somehow, that if I moved I would break it, that it would shatter all around me in bright shards. So I lay there as still as I could, in a kind of child's game, waiting for the right moment to break the seal on my day.

Oh Lord, I thought, in the drowsy misjudgment of morning. How could I have gotten it so wrong?

I remember the window cast a bluish square of sun, a cage, in the corner of my room and I imagined it moving across the whole of the floor, the bed, the pillow, through the first day of my life alone. A stillness. As if all the dust from a life's movement had settled years ago. Not a sound from anywhere; not a sound from that other room, which I imagined as empty of every tie and shoe I'd ever bought him. I pictured it, the mirror of my room: all white with sheets piled up in the corner and an ashtray left full after a night of packing and talking and loading a life into a car. Maybe he sat alone in there and wept. I can't say. But how could you not weep? How could you not wish you'd done things a little better from the start?

And out front, beyond the walls of the house, I imagined the space where a stain of oil was all that would be left of Buzz's new car. I saw the car climbing a hill in the deep silent fog, and then turning onto Market Street, those two smoking a shared pack of cigarettes and one—probably my husband—asking if the other had a light. Then off across the bridge, the fog gradually lifting as they entered Oakland, and where would they be now? Tracy. Livermore. Altamont. Out in the farmlands with sunlight breaking on a lake top all at once, and green around them as far as they could see.

A dog began barking. From outside came the clink of bottles on the step. The new seltzer boy. Now that war had crippled the old seltzer boy. It was enough.

I sat up, put on my robe, and walked through the hall. My head was still clouded from the pill, packed in cotton. Holland's door was open and I could see a slice of what I'd pictured: the bed neat and careful. His shade was up and the day lay bare before me. So they were gone.

I went to my son's room and found every bit of him hidden under blankets; I had a brief panic that, like a jailbreak in a movie, the bed was stuffed with pillows in the shape of a boy . . . then a bare foot jerked out of the covers, and I was calmed. I woke him the same as if it were any morning—"Good morning, gingerbread baby"—kissing each eye awake and he struggled, fists to his eyes like a boxer, as I lifted him out of the bed and onto his feet. I stroked Sonny's weary forehead as I did every morning.

I felt them gone. It was all so matter-of-fact: a light left on in the living room, a pillow on the floor for some reason, a glass of bourbon spilled then righted on the table. They must have left in a hurry, I thought to myself; I took a nearby towel (red-stained) and soaked up the booze until its cold touched my palm. I could almost smell coffee. Sonny made a sound in the bedroom and the birds made a sound in the yard. I brought up the shades—bright sunless day!—and vine fingers trailed down from the gutter, as if ready to lift the very roof off the house at my command.

You had done it, I thought. You had left me. And despite everything I had been through and planned, all the walks on the foggy boardwalk, the pain I had worked to unknot and release, still—a shock—it felt like a rock thrown through my window, smashing everything to splinters, without even a note tied to it. Faithless man. Coward. I knew what I had said and done to force your decision. Though I was the one who revealed your war story, gave the plan for your seduction, plucked away the girl's temptations, rehearsed this very morning, this moment, for hours every day, still the blame fell suddenly on you. Was it so desperate here with me? With Sonny? Was life so sad, Holland, hope so meager that some buried ember, some last spark, might not be dug up in the morning light to start a new fire? I was prepared for solitude— even for freedom—but I was not prepared for this: the abandonment. I had hidden that away in a room within me, the shade shut so I would never see it. Now it was out, and I wept. I knelt on the floor of my living room and wept. Not just for the parts I had been ready to lose, the years, not just for what I had done. But, in the end, for what you had done. We want to think we cling to people as they try to leave, attach to them like thorns, so that they stay. We must stay for each other, I thought, absurdly. We must. What else is all the talk, and love and kindness for?

Again, my awakening thought: Had I missed it all? Everything you had tried to tell me. Was it all as upside down as a hall of mirrors? The look of fear when you stepped into that circle of light and saw me standing with Buzz Drumer, that relic perhaps of a love gone cold; the careful speech you prepared before the air-raid siren wailed; the night at the Rose Bowl when you danced as if to woo me; the look, that day in the hall, of peace, of a man who had made a decision. Perhaps I had not understood you, after all. What did you want? Did you ever really tell me?

I had not fought for you, in all my dealings with Buzz. I had not known how and, in the end, I had given up the thought forever. And yet in the morning light as I lay motionless in bed, it had occurred to me—madly, foolishly—that you might not be gone. A reckless thought. That after everything, Holland, you might stay.

You do not judge a man by what he says. You judge him by what he does. What did I weep for that morning? When the light was beautiful, and wealth and a new life spread before me, my son laughing from the kitchen? It was that fantasy, a foolish one: that even after the last bell rang, you finally had fought for me. I wept to know, once and for all, that you had not.

I pulled myself together. I closed the door in my mind that led down that lonely hall; I would try it again later, alone. But that morning, I had a child to deal with, to explain things to, and a life to begin. I straightened the room as Lyle came back in and sniffed at the trail of old lovers: the pillow, the table, the towel. I blinked at the fog-bound sun, and the confused cherry trees down the sidewalk, always blooming at the wrong time. The window of a parked car, engine running, ruby lights glowing, revealed a brunette staring at me; a moment later she was gone. I heard Sonny, in the kitchen, asking for milk. I began to clean the room, picking up the towel and the glass.

I walked down the hall and toward the kitchen. As I rounded the corner, Sonny looked at me brightly.

"Hi Mama," he said. "Lyle won't come out."

I stood still for a moment. "Sweetheart?" He had a cup of milk in his hand.

"Here, Lyle! He won't come, Mama. He's under the table."

"Where'd you get that, sweetheart?"

He said that it was Daddy.

"What do you mean?"

My son looked at me quizzically, then turned away. I followed his eyes into the room and it stopped my heart. The sugar cube. For there I saw, above his morning coffee, bruised and broken, the cautious smile of my husband's face.

There are many worlds, they say, for our many choices. In one, my husband walked out from our house in darkness, stepped into that car, and was taken forever from his old life. A ride across the country in a DeSoto, with every new horizon forgetting, just a little, what he had left behind; forgiving me a little for what I had taken in exchange. One in which he found a flat in New York City, and lived with his lover with a view of a skyline like a lowered chandelier, where they banged the steam pipes for heat in winter and opened the windows for air in summer, with fights and reconciliations and trouble: a lifelong love. Letters and visits to his son, phone calls and photographs in the mail. One in which Pearlie Cook raised that son on five hundred acres north of San Francisco, sent him to Harvard, and traveled on a boat to all the places she had read about in books. One in which this is Buzz's love story, somewhere out there.

But I only know this world. The one in which I lived in my house, with my son and husband and our debts. In which a man came one night and fought with my husband—fought to the point of fists—this time my husband's broken nose, his blood on a towel, so that the man drove away and did not return. The world in which that summer night my husband fought and stayed, and not for fear or stubbornness or confusion, but for his one passion, despite everything. This is my story. In which he stayed for me.

What is one to make of love?

All the real moments of my life took place in that vine-covered house. It was in that living room, only a year later, that our buzzing radio brought news of a desegregated South, colored folks refusing to ride the buses in Montgomery, people marching everywhere, sick and tired of it at last. It came through the lyre-shaped mouth as if from the lips of an oracle. It told of how Senator McCarthy had been humiliated in front of the Army Sub-committee, and later of his death. The world was changing, all around us, and out on the ocean we felt it as the farthest edge of a whip feels its movement. It was in that hallway, opening the mail, that I learned my son would go to college on a scholarship, far away in New York City; it was there I hugged him goodbye and then fell into my husband's arms and wept. After his gradua-tion, at that kitchen table, I pulled Sonny's draft notice from its official envelope. I held it in my hands and wondered at the cycle of things. Boys not wanting to die, mothers not wanting to lose them. I took a rusty thumbtack and pinned it to the wall, then called my son and told him what to do.

This is a story of men not going to war, a story of other battles. Sonny did not go to war, but he did fight. He fought on his cam-pus; he fought hard, and tried to shout down the war, tried to burn it down. When a bomb went off it was blamed on his group, though I don't believe he had anything to do with it; his "group" was never anything more than some kids convinced that it all had to come down, and one or two of them took it too far. He fled to Canada, where he stayed a long time, until Carter called all of the draft dodgers back, and Sonny—now Walter—came home bring-ing a tall, skinny Chinese girl with a high permed hairdo. She was pregnant. And so the fights with Holland began.

"You and Mama don't know what I been through!" my son said.

Holland shook his head and would not look at him.

"You never been through hard times! You never stood up and fought for *nothing*!"

I said that was enough. I could not tell him the story of how, in six months of madness, his father had stood up and fought for me. I only said he'd been to war. That didn't impress my son at all, and the skinny girl had nothing to say about any of it; she stood there with her hand on her belly, staring at the broken mantel clock. She disappeared, a week later, along with the grandchild I never saw.

Sonny left for New York City, calling me every week or so, and it was in that house, on the chair that replaced the old worn telephone bench, I heard that he and his new girlfriend, Lucy, had married. I nervously told Holland and he chuckled, so I took it as a cue to laugh with him. At the divide that separated us from our son, at the impetuosity of young men, and women; at the eternal urge of love itself. I saw, out that front window, as faces in the neighborhood changed from Irish to Filipino and Chinese, and foreign music played from yards on warm nights, and foreign scents came over the old sand-scarred garden fences. It was in that hall I heard the shivering sound of the last milk bottle delivered to my doorstep. And it was there, on that table, I dropped my purse when I came home from the hospital, the night that Holland died.

His kidneys had turned on him, hardening, refusing to work, like servants with drawn daggers. He spent his final days in the hospital, buoyed by morphine, and the doctors assured me he felt no pain. His face revealed a man at peace, looking around the last room of his life. No pain. Only once did we ever mention that night long ago, and then only briefly; those six months in a long marriage had become like a small figure in a wide mural. Sonny flew out from New York for the funeral, and he stayed in his father's room, because his childhood room had been converted for sewing and storage. I think that affected him deeply, to sleep in his father's old bed, with his shoes still standing in the closet. We

spent a few days going through the boxes, and eventually I gave
the whole task over to my son. A man came to have me sign some
forms for organ donation. It was a such a strange thing to have to
do, but apparently my husband had arranged it long before. Later
they informed me Holland's heart was a curiosity. A curiosity.
Well aren't they all?

He was buried in a military funeral in Colma, and some old
Sunset friends, like my neighbor Edith, paid their respects. Holland's only relative to attend, besides Sonny, was Alice, the surviving aunt, sadly regal in her wheelchair and her wig, her left
hand shaking like an aspen. I wonder what caused that private
smile she wore. I wonder if she remembered telling me not to
marry him. Despite their fights, Sonny mourned his father keenly,
and I, holding his hand as the preacher spoke, could not hide my
own desperate tears.

It was many years later that my grandson's voice came over the
telephone in my new apartment. Decades had passed since the operator would come on first, announcing: "Long distance, please
hold." I was in my seventies by then; the first time I realized my age
was when I tried on a scarf in San Francisco and said it was a little
bright for an old woman like me, expecting the clerk to contradict
me—"You're not old!"—and when he didn't, I saw myself at last
for what I was. An old woman. I have to say I laughed out loud.

"Nana?"

"Perry, did you get over your cold?"

"Olive has it now," he announced to me, meaning his stuffed
bear who was as real to him as his mother or me. Or else as imaginary. "It's bad."

We talked a little while about his bear and about his mother
before there was a fumble on the line and my son came on:

"I'm going to be in town, Mama, next week for a conference

of NGOs and donors." He was the president now of a large non-profit in New York.

"Are you bringing Lucy and Perry?"

"No, it's too much trouble."

"I've got to clean up the guest room—" I began. I had long since moved out of the Cook house in the Sunset into a part of town where everything was delivered. Just like the old bread wagon, the egg lady, the milkman, and the seltzer boy. Strange how the past returns in different clothes, pretending to be a stranger.

"Oh," he said and I heard him pause. "They've got a room for me at the hotel. All the meetings are going on there, Mama."

"Of course." I bristled at the duty that "Mama" implied.

"Why don't you come and see me there? We could have breakfast on the twelfth."

"I'd love that."

"The St. Francis."

"I'd better air out my good dress," I said and he laughed. Lucy came on for a moment to tell me about something she had read in the news and thought would infuriate me, which it did, and we chatted for a moment in self-righteous agreement. She was a white girl, and merciless when it came to the failings of her race. I liked her very much.

I took the early streetcar downtown, because I never went there anymore, and stood across the street from the St. Francis, looking around Union Square. The tall buildings surrounded it cozily, brightened by the signs of shops that had come from New York or Europe to claim a view on the square. One of the last remaining cable cars clanged by, headed uphill. People sat on steps drinking coffee or eating pastries from bags, watching a street performer: a boy who had painted himself in gold. Nothing remained of the former square except the single pillar in the middle, the bronze woman atop it, celebrating Dewey's triumph in the Pacific. From that angle, I could see the old luncheon spot and, in the window, I imagined myself viewed through a fracture in time, being advised by two older women about my forthcoming marriage: "Don't marry him!" The cycle of things. For surely that young woman, taking a popover from the waiter, would nod her head and smile. And go and marry him anyway.

Sonny was shyly ironic about being in his hometown, dressed so handsomely in a suit and tie, seated before a glass of champagne with his mother. "You wouldn't know I'd blown up a post office," he joked. I said he never blew up anything, and he shrugged. We were in the hotel restaurant, which sat slightly above the lobby, separated only by some palms and a brief set of stairs. Beyond the lobby's elevators and groupings of leather chairs, we could see the hotel's main entrance, and behind us another glass door led from the restaurant onto the street, where city life passed by in bright sunlight. I told the waitress that my son was an important man here for a conference, and he hid his face in his napkin. To hide the joy at his own success. He knew how proud I was.

Almost as soon as the waitress left, he leaned forward and asked: "Mama, who is Charles Drumer?"

I straightened in my chair and fiddled with my napkin, trying to calm the wave of warmth rising in me. I took in a long deep breath. A woman sitting across from us began to laugh. "That's right," I said. "His name was Charles. You don't remember him?"

"A white man visiting our house? I'm sure I'd remember that."

"Well."

"Is he a secret from your past?"

"I don't know what you mean." I was trying to hold myself perfectly still.

"I bet you don't! I was at a reception last week for this event, I spoke for a bit about housing, and a man came up to me and asked if I was the son of Holland and Pearlie Cook. He didn't explain anything about himself. I said I was, and he handed me an envelope. He must have written it when I was talking. Here it is."

He produced a piece of cream stationery, with my name printed in shaky handwriting. "I found out later he's a major donor, so I was glad I was polite."

"Of course you were polite," I said, picking up the envelope.

"I read it," Sonny admitted, smiling. "It just says to meet him here in the lobby."

My hand began to shake, and my silverware fell to the floor with a shattering sound. My son said it was all right, he would get it—and looked at me warily.

"Are you okay, Mama?"

"He's here?" I opened the envelope.

"Of course he is. It was a reception for this conference." *I would love to see you . . . I'll be in the St. Francis lobby at ten thirty.* It was nearly ten.

"I have to go," I whispered, but my son gave me a sour look as our food arrived.

"Who is he, Mama? You don't have to be so careful. Dad's dead, nobody minds anymore these days. You were young. I can guess what must have gone on."

"Don't be silly."

He leaned over. "Was he the one you almost threw everything over for?"

Sharply: "Did your father say something?"

Sonny smiled. "It wouldn't surprise me if you had some man, years ago . . ."

I rarely thought of him in all that time. When I did, it was with the distant fondness of a childhood friend. I had no photographs; he had slipped out of our lives completely. Of course Sonny couldn't remember the man who had visited our house for six months when he was little, the summer Lyle ran away. I was the only witness still alive, and so it was almost as if I had imagined Buzz. From the few newspaper items that found their way to me over the years, I learned he lived in New York, so the city took on the air of being *his* city. A party with drinks on a grand piano, a balcony with a view, a famous man in a corner, an infamous woman in the elevator. And, leaning over the railing with Buzz, a new lover. In my imagination, he had found happiness after all. He must have. How startling to feel him come alive again, in his hotel room, already straightening his tie before a mirror, and if he were to walk out of one of those elevators it would be like a character stepping out of the pages of an old, tattered book.

"Yes," I said quietly. "Yes, he was the one."

"Aha! Tell me about this old lover of yours—"

"What was he like?"

"You're avoiding the question! Nice, happy enough. You'll see for yourself." The check arrived, and he gave them his room number, and then stood to leave. "Should I stay?"

He was longing to step into my past. "No, go on up." I looked down at myself, my old flowered dress. "I can't meet him like this."

"It doesn't matter, Mama," he said. "He's an old man." And by that I understood that I was an old woman, and vanity was years behind me.

I was left alone in the restaurant, with the remains of our breakfasts and the attendant vase of daffodils, trumpets on high. The laughing woman was leaving with her party, heading out through the glass door to the street, but on the other side of the room stairs led down to the lobby, where those discreet pairings of leather chairs implied old-fashioned rendezvous and not the business appointments which were their current fate. I wondered what this seemed like to my son. The thwarted passions of another age; the fetters of a tragic time. As if his own time were the perfect one in which to be born, his choices utterly free, his life without a single regret—as if he didn't have an illegitimate child who might even now be judging those choices seemingly made in another era. He was a man of fifty. Even his generation was ceding to the next.

My mind had wandered; there, in one of the lobby chairs facing away from me, I saw the neatly parted white hair of a man. He must have entered the moment before. A tall man, in an expensive gray suit, leaning toward the flower arrangement. What was this hurry in my heart?

Holland only mentioned his name once. We were at a memorial benefit hosted by a successful colored woman. It was sometime in the 1980s, in Sausalito, across the bay near where the Rose Bowl used to be, high on a hill overlooking the water and the dark outline of Angel Island. No house blocked her view; she owned the grove below her. For all that, it was a casual party of few pretensions, not especially either staid or raucous—it was, after all, to fund a memorial scholarship—so I was surprised, when it was time to leave, that Holland handed me the car keys and said he was in no position to drive. Not until that moment did I realize he was drunk.

He stood on the garden path, among the fragrant tuberoses, leaning against the gate and staring at the view. In the moonlight, his silhouette was the same at nearly sixty as in his teens. Age had taken none of his charm, his beauty; he had instead patinaed like old bronze. In his eyes, I saw that look of blindness that overtakes the old, who stand and stare at a tree or a house, unseeing; just the simple experience of memory.

"I'm sorry," he said, holding on to the gate for support. I wondered how many glasses of champagne he'd had, and whether anyone else had noticed. My mind was still on the party, the plump charming hostess, the businessmen and their wives and what they thought of us, the Cooks. An unseen boat rang its bell on the water.

"It's all right, you had a good time. I didn't notice you drinking," I said.

"No," he said, shaking his head. "I'm sorry I couldn't do it."

I didn't know what he meant.

He motioned to the house and the view, and his gesture included the tuberoses, the path, the moonlight and dark island before us. "I couldn't give you all this."

I laughed. "Well of course not! Let's get you—"

"I should have!" he stated, blinking. "I should have let him give it all to you!" Then he shook his head. "But I couldn't do it. I'm sorry. I know it's what you wanted."

That was when, out of nowhere, softly, surprisingly, with a pop on the first consonant and a hum on the last, my husband said a name I had not heard in thirty years.

Neither of us changed position: him looking out at the water, me looking at him. We were as quiet as parents in the room of a sleeping child. The clamor of the party was muffled behind the flowering bushes, and from an open window floated the sound of piano playing. I watched my husband as he listened.

"I did not want it," I said.

His face turned slowly and surprised me. It was fixed in bewilderment. Of course it was. After all of our years, all my work to understand him, in the end, I was the greater mystery. The inexplicable Pearlie Cook. There was no fathoming the girl who sat by him in the dark room of his mother's house; who found him on a beach; who clipped his paper and bought a barkless dog and a bell that cooed instead of rang. A glove with a bird in the hand. What a series of riddles! The whole episode, from the moment he saw me with Buzz in that living room until that night, sitting beside him by the radio, when he looked at me to ask what I wanted and I said nothing to stop him. Sitting with a glass of bourbon, his hand making the ice shake. And no word from me, no struggle. To have his first love—the girl he stared at in school and whose hand he took on a walk along the road to Childress, the girl for whom he committed a crime so he would not have to leave her—to have her say "Goodbye" and know that in an hour it would be over. What a lonely hour. How had I missed it? All those years of marriage, I thought I was studying him, but the entire time he was watching me more carefully, more ardently; like an old Kentucky dowser, stepping across the dry land with a forked branch, waiting for some sign of what lay deep below. The source of me. And all those years, poor man, he got me wrong.

"It was all for you," I said quietly. "You wanted it, I was sure."
We think we know the ones we love.

In his eyes I saw the doubt of many years resolving. "No," he said at last. "No, I never did."

There we stood, in the warm scent of the garden, the piano music drifting in. Around us spread the black water, the blacker island, and the years of misunderstandings and doubt. We stood looking at each other for a very long time. There would be more evenings like this, with the moon passing from the trees and the fog held back by the bridge like a curtain. Beautiful evenings, with Holland looking up at me with the moonlight on him. There would be more parties, more drinks and wanderings to find the car, more flowers, more boats, more bells, more death. More and more and more, until his kidneys turned on him at last. And it was I, the widow, who would choose what to put on his gravestone: that he was loyal, and decent, and served his country in a war. That is what Holland would have written down for you, and it is what I wrote for the stonemason. Just that. And if you came to see that grave, you might walk away and think it all dead ground without a flower. You would never guess.

"Take my arm," I said at last, and he leaned on me as I guided him toward the gate. There would be more. But we would never talk about the past again. We had closed it up like a house too big and drafty for old people to live in, and instead we lived in the small warm place our marriage had made.

"This way," I said, and he followed.

The hotel lobby, the man in the chair: one moment it was my old friend, and the next it was not. A mangled hand pulling out one of the flowers; or no, a play of light. Through the swinging door, I could see gingko trees blooming along the street and a silver balloon in one, almost within reach; a young man in a hat stretched for it, a girl watching expectantly beside him. I looked back at the man in the gray suit, still waiting. It was him. I stood up from my seat.

It had been folly for Buzz to think he could force old love to return exactly as it was. Just like the sensation of awakening in the middle of the night, torn out of a pleasant dream. You try to thread yourself back into that dream. You convince yourself it can be done: you close your eyes, remembering just where you left off—a rosebush, a picnic, a long-dead mother. So you fall asleep, and sink into a dream—but never, never back into *that* dream. It is always gone forever. For we can no more revive old love than we can return to that awakened dream.

An old love, an old friend. The man in the chair; I knew so little of his life. A wealthy man in New York City, a political donor, sitting in a room full of other well-dressed men, laughing, and a lover's hand on his knee, patting it gently. He could not have thought of me much in that time, not with people, worries, illnesses, and death. No more than I had thought of him. And now, to revive it all.

Some do try. Is it folly—or the best use of our lives to try?

I would walk down those three steps to the lobby and approach the chair. I would wait for a moment behind him, steadying myself, feeling the strange contraction of time taking place. A hurry in the heart. Then I would step into view—*Hello, Buzz*—and he would rise in astonishment—*Look at you!*—and we would both laugh at how the years had altered us, and everything around, and left us here, just as many travelers had laughed before us, meeting overseas and finding each other in this very lobby, these same worn leather chairs. We would embrace, and talk about our present lives, happy enough. That slightly broken nose, those sapphirine eyes still flashing, his hand on mine. And then we would talk about the past. *I'm sure Sonny told you that Holland died.* An old wound, like shrapnel, would twist inside us both. An old door, bricked up and plastered over years ago, would be revealed again; another life; each of us would stare at it, move our hands along the surface until we could feel the edges.

So we would come around at last to the real purpose of his

note. I'm sure seeing my son's name at a fund-raiser was a shock and delight to old Buzz; surely it seemed like a chance, in old age, not to be missed. The little boy, grown into middle age, who did not remember him. An innocent conversation, some harmless prying into the past, and then the note, an impetuous leap. I'm sure he took pleasure in the thought of seeing me, his old accomplice in a failed endeavor, just to go to that memory once again and this time touch the bottom. But he had not come all that way merely to see my face. He had come, I knew, to put an old question to rest. Sitting before me and smiling, a tremor in his one good hand, old age nearly disguising him. But I could not answer it for him. I couldn't say: *In the end, he loved me more.* That would not be kind, or even really true. Leaning forward in his chair, those blue eyes fixed on me: "Tell me, Pearlie, why did Holland do it? Why did he stay?"

How could I possibly explain my marriage? Anyone watching a ship from land is no judge of its seaworthiness, for the vital part is always underwater. It can't be seen.

Why did he do it? we ask of the conventional professor who runs off with his student. And of the doting girl who breaks her engagement: *Why didn't she?* It's what we always ask of others' lives. Luck was all before them, fortune and happiness; for some reason they turned and stepped off the precipice. What vision did they see there? Passion and beauty explain nothing—these stories are everywhere, and few of us are beautiful. The balance tilts both rich and poor. It might be the folly of youth, or the whims of old age, but this madness does not discriminate: an old widower about to remarry might change his mind, his middle-aged children in the pews, and be unable to state his reason. What could he say that would not sound like folly? We think we know people, and dismiss the scenes as aberrations, as the lightning strikes of madness, but surely we are wrong. Surely these are the truest moments of their lives. Why did that old man in the chair, Buzz Drumer, sell off his family's property, and fortune, and legacy to be with one man, long ago? Why did my husband, at the last hour, stay rather than leave? We cannot know until one day the vision appears to us: that chances are few, and death comes soon enough. Take rapture if it's in your grasp; take love if you can reach it. For Buzz, the love was Holland. For Holland, it was Sonny and me. Not madness. Perhaps: in commonplace lives, our single act of poetry.

"Happy enough," my son had said.

I sat a long time at my table. People came and went but the old man waited in his chair. Out of the corner of my eye, I saw the silver balloon dip low and the young man leap to catch it. The girl beside him clapped each time he did this, jumping fruitlessly, once, twice, arm stretched to the sky. And then, losing his hat, he caught it. He pulled it down. He handed it to the girl beside him, laughing. At that, as if it were the signal I was looking for, I stood and walked to the door, stepping out into the startling day.